I Have Friends in Heaven

NOVELS BY

MAX CATTO

The Flanagan Boy
The Killing Frost
The Sickle
A Prize of Gold
The Mummers
Gold in the Sky
The Devil at Four O'Clock
The Melody of Sex
Mister Moses
The Tiger in the Bed
D-Day in Paradise
Love From Venus
I Have Friends in Heaven

I Have Friends in Heaven

Max Catto

LITTLE, BROWN AND COMPANY · BOSTON · TORONTO

FOR

DWYE EVANS

WITH GOOD REASON

I

HE was as stringy as a hungry cat. He was tall for his age. But docks are made for criminally-minded men, not boys, and he had to stand on a box to see properly over the top.

He stared at the magistrate. The magistrate stared back.

The village of Lorenzo of the Angels was too poor to afford a magistrate of its own. So this one came in once a fortnight from the town of San Cosimo, which was a three-hour truck drive over the mountains, or eight hours on the back of a mule. The scenery was wild and magnificent. For some perverse reason this magistrate preferred the back of the mule.

He was a kindly man. He was a school-teacher, too, which meant that he understood children. And he stared at the boy in the dock, thinking: he doesn't have Italian eyes. They were cool and grey and wary. Italian boys' eyes burned. A long cowlick of flaxen hair drooped over a broad white brow. Italian hair tended to be black and curly, like burnished wire-wool.

There is something a little mixed-up about this boy. I hope he hasn't been so mixed-up as to do something very bad.

Well, we will soon find out. The magistrate banged his gavel on the bench to declare the court open, and as he did so a very fat man leapt to his feet, as if the bang had released a spring under his buttocks, and shouted emotionally, 'Let justice be done.'

Luigi Pirelli, the fake antique dealer. 'It will be,' the magistrate said, giving him a cold look. He had once bought a Medici chair from him, and it turned out to have been made in Luigi's shop four centuries after most of the Medicis were dust in their tombs. An antique-fixer. A driller of worm-holes in new wood, and a tarnisher and rubber of factory brass to make it look old. It was going to be hard to dispense justice impartially.

Luigi clawed at the air to command attention. 'Mister Magistrate,' he cried.

'Sit down. And wait until you are called.'

'Why waste time? Call me now.'

'Will you be quiet?'

'My blood has been shed.' Luigi's arms whirled and he formed his index fingers and thumbs into a theatrical frame about a piece of sticking plaster on his brow.

'Who has shed it?'

'The monster in the dock.'

'Monster?' the magistrate said with pity. 'He is hardly more than a child.'

Luigi said sufferingly, 'I throw myself on the mercy of the court.' And his arms shot up in an heroic gesture of supplication. Fingers splayed and trembling slightly. Pointed accusingly at God.

He was a hand-talker. Most Italians use their fingers to bring out the subtlety of the language. But Luigi was something rather spectacular. By the time he had finished patting and slapping his words they seemed to come out of his mouth in a different shape. He used all the traditional gestures: but electrically. His wrists were miracles of elucidation. Each elbow was as vocal as a trained actor.

Luigi's wife now rose in the well of the court and she yelled, 'Justice.' She was a squat wrestler of a woman with a marked moustache. Her ill-favoured daughter, Sophia, rose too. 'Justice,' she cried.

Look at them. Luigi's trained seals.

The boy in the dock watched them disdainfully. His lips

2

formed two scathing words, but he didn't let them be heard in the court. He caught the magistrate's humorous glance. He does not seem a bad man. But you have to be careful with authority. All bureaucrats are alike.

'Everybody silent,' the magistrate said. And he went to the window to look out. There was something wrong with the weather and he couldn't be quite sure what it was. Something terribly still about the air. The sun glared on the barren hills. How quiet it was. As if something unpleasant impended.

Rain? No. Nothing but that scorching glitter in the sky. The magistrate wiped his neck and went back to the bench.

I wish the mule had thrown a shoe. Or I had had a slight attack of dysentery to keep me at home.

'Let the prisoner's parents come forward,' he said, glancing at the boy in the dock.

How old was he? Twelve? Thirteen?

'There is nobody,' the policeman of the village of Lorenzo of the Angels said.

'Nobody?'

'He is an orphan.'

'Ah. What is his name?'

'Caesar.'

'A name of some reputation. Caesar what?'

'Caesar nothing.'

The magistrate said exasperatedly, 'He must be called *something*.'

'He is fatherless.'

'A bastard,' the priest said, rising unasked in the court. He was a thin harsh man and he used the word in a particularly virulent way as if determined that the fruit of an act of physical passion should bear the guilt of the sin. The fathers have eaten sour grapes, according to the bible, and the children's teeth are set on edge. Priests shouldn't talk like that, the magistrate thought.

3

'Some English soldier,' the priest said bitterly. 'You know how it was.'

So that accounts for the fair hair.

'The mother died when he was five,' the priest said.

The boy in the dock looked at him with disgust.

This is a young man of passionate independence. I like him. I cannot see his legs but I am sure they are planted squarely on the ground, the magistrate thought.

'How has he lived?' he asked.

'In the gutter. Nobody let him starve.'

But nobody let him live with respect for humanity.

'He is good with machines. He helps on the farms,' the policeman said. 'He asks for no charity. He has made a home in the corner of Luigi's shed. It is not bad. There are even pictures on the wall.'

'A palace,' Luigi said piously. 'For which I charge him only a thousand lire a month.'

'I applaud your benevolence,' the magistrate said, thinking: sit down, Shylock. You make me sick. He stared hard at the boy. The cool grey eyes were marvellously self-possessed.

The boy thought: how these grown-ups talk. I could have told them the facts in half as many words. For instance, that Luigi's shed, which is my palace, lets in the rain, and there are rats, which frankly I prefer to Luigi. And it isn't a thousand lire a month. Luigi is a congenital liar. Congenital is a good word. I must remember it. I pay that fat cheat with the moustachio'd wife and the sniffling daughter fifteen hundred lire a month.

The magistrate mused: he is thinking something insulting. I am probably included. Never mind. He has the right to insult human beings in his thoughts.

He said in a kind voice, 'Your interests will be protected, Caesar.'

'I am capable of protecting them myself,' Caesar said indifferently.

4

The magistrate swallowed.

'No offence was intended,' Caesar said.

'I am glad to hear it,' the magistrate said.

He peered out again. There *is* something wrong with the weather today. It's so hard to breathe. The sun was a very strange colour. It seemed to press down on the earth like a hot copper lid. And the uncanny stillness. The ticking of the clock was thunderous on the wall. He said to the policeman, 'Are you aware of something odd?'

'Only the heat.'

'Something else.'

'My stomach rumbling?'

Idiot.

Caesar said softly, 'The birds have stopped singing. I cannot hear an animal grumbling. They are afraid to open their mouths.'

The magistrate congratulated him with a nod. 'Your perceptions are very acute.'

'Perhaps they will come in useful in prison,' Caesar said with a chuckle, 'if you put me away for seven years.'

'Am I going to?'

'I hope not. I have a lot to do. There is no time to waste,' Caesar said.

It surprised the magistrate. 'What is your hurry?'

'I am twelve. Almost thirteen. I have to grow up quickly. I am going to make my mark in the world,' the boy said.

The magistrate studied him fixedly. He beckoned to the policeman. 'Fetch him in front of the dock. Let me see him,' he said.

The boy got off the box and came round. The magistrate looked at the ragged pants. I guessed right. He *does* have good staunch legs. He looked at the incongruous flaxen hair, remembering Pope Gregory's words when he first set eyes on the young Anglo-Saxon captives. *Non Angli sed Angeli*. Not Angles but angels. This one is probably no

5

angel. He chuckled back at the boy, 'I do not even know what frightful crime you have committed.'

'Assault,' Luigi burst out, three fingers splayed to express pain, indignation and shock. Then he crooked his knuckles, shouting, 'Assault with blood.' In some strange way the twisted hands suggested the colour of blood.

The magistrate thought wearily: oh, stop it. Your dramatics are making me sweat.

And again he peered peculiarly out of the window. The electricity in the air was tense. Not a leaf trembled. The trees as still as if painted. What *was* the matter with the animals? Not a cow, not a goat, not a bird to be heard. It was unnerving. And that queer, flaming, copper-coloured sky. If it came down any closer it would set the world on fire.

The priest said suddenly in his thin, cruel voice, 'He does not go to church.' The accusation seemed for an odd moment to be connected with the unpleasantness outside.

'Who? The boy?'

'He has never attended Mass. Not once in all these years.'

'Has he been asked?'

'God does not ask for the discipline of religion. It is demanded.'

The magistrate wasn't an outright agnostic, but he wasn't much of a church-goer either. He had to be careful.

'He is a pagan,' the priest said.

'He isn't being tried for not going to church,' the magistrate said.

And then something – well, biblical – happened. He felt a fuzzed sensation as if the roots of the earth had slipped. His vision blurred for an instant. The bench seemed to move slightly as if a straining animal were underneath. Then it was over. It had only lasted a fraction of a second. But he had heard a faint click and everybody looked up at the picture of Garibaldi on the wall. The glass had split.

6

The magistrate went to the window to stare out. The landscape hadn't changed. It was still oven-hot. And terribly silent. The distant blue mountains were still there and the little stream ran down the culvert of the village as before. He wiped the sweat off his neck and said unconvincingly, 'It is nothing. It is a very old building. The foundations have settled.' He lost his goose-pimples. He looked at the boy who had never been to church. 'Let us get on with the case,' he said.

The policeman began to recite, 'At eleven minutes before midday on . . .'

'Do we have to get chronological? In this heat?'

'He is charged under the law of Victor Emmanuel the Second . . .'

'He has been dead a long time. He is no longer interested.' Something had given the magistrate a headache. 'Let the boy tell me.'

'I am supposed to have stolen my own head,' the boy said.

Is he making fun of me? The magistrate stiffened. 'Your *what*?'

'The policeman has it. My marble head.'

'Mine,' Luigi erupted. His anguish was frightful. He mimed it with his wrists, flapping them like the wings of a wounded bird, and everybody in the courtroom caught his breath. Except the magistrate. He was getting tired of the performance.

He banged his gavel. 'Be quiet——' he almost said 'actor'.

The policeman placed a small marble head on the bench.

The magistrate handled it with awe. It was hardly bigger than a medium-sized melon. Age had given it a lovely patina. It had also chipped a few morsels off the smooth brow. The magistrate recognized the features at once. He looked at the sightless virile masculine face, the short dominant nose. He could decipher the faint inscription on

7

the base, CAESAR IMPERATO – where a piece of the plinth was broken off. Probably it had once adorned the home of some forgotten Tribune. It might even have been a gift to the mighty Caesar himself.

He gave the boy a searching look and said, 'Where did you get it?'

'Up in the hills. Where the ruins are.'

The magistrate knew about the ruins. They probably dated back to Vespasian.

'Tell me,' he said.

The boy hesitated proudly. As if resenting having to justify himself. Then he said, 'He asked me to fetch in his goats.' He glanced at Luigi, twitching like a decapitated chicken. 'He said he would pay me fifty lire.' The boy shrugged with contempt. 'He didn't.' He went on, 'They were up by the ruins.' He could remember everything very clearly. There were four goats. Each as cross-grained and emotional as Luigi. They were nibbling amongst the old grey stones and the remains of the mosaic pavements. Caesar spent ten breathless minutes rounding three of them up.

The fourth was as ancient as Methuselah. And fifty times as agile. In the end Caesar cornered it against a stone pillar and he seized the long senile beard and said irritably, 'Stop playing games. I am no cowboy.' He would never have suspected the old fool of such energy. It leapt clean over the pillar with one violent 'Me-eh', and Caesar, still clinging to the beard, was dragged in an avalanche of stones and earth down the hill. They both ended up in the stream. The goat chuckled and joined his friends. Caesar rubbed his grazed knee, examining his torn pants. They were the only ones he possessed.

It was in this rueful mood that he saw a face staring straight at him from the ripples of the stream. They eddied about a clear white brow and a proud sensual mouth. He thought for a moment that it was a trick of the water. He put his hand under it and touched smooth stone. He felt a queer sharp thrill. He examined the face, and the ageless masterful eyes examined him. The water had washed off the earth that had secreted it for fifteen centuries and he scrubbed the broken plinth and read the inscription: CAESAR IMPERATO – mutilated of its final 'R'.

The first strange thought that entered his mind was: my name, too. I am no IMPERATOR. But this is no coincidence. His excitement grew and grew until it almost choked him. He stroked the marble cheeks, feeling the round strong chin and the assertive nose. Then he ran his fingers over his own chin and nose. He thought: we have the same face.

At this point of Caesar's story the startled magistrate peered at him, then at the marble. He wondered: is it possible that there *is* some resemblance? He is talking himself into it. He is talking me into it, too.

And then the even stranger thought entered Caesar's mind: it is me. I am the living resurrection of this stone. Of course, he wasn't capable of putting his emotions into such fanciful language. He thought quite simply: I am the child of this man.

He has lain there in the darkness, century after century, waiting patiently for my hand. My hand, only. It is *me*.

The magistrate stared fascinatedly at the obsessed young ardent face. He didn't interrupt him. He let him go on.

Caesar wrapped the head carefully in his shirt. He knew that in that instant, for some reason that was vaguely beyond him, his whole life had changed. He shouted to the goats, and they all went back to Luigi's shed. A dark corner of it was his home. His bed was a canvas sack of straw. A charitable soul in the village had donated the blankets. There was a bench and a small stove on which he cooked. Even two pictures. Caesar had worked for these. He sat in the sunshine, polishing the marble tenderly with his spit.

A shadow fell on him. Luigi was staring down at him. His face was very covetous. He said huskily, 'What have you got there?'

'I found it.'

'Here?'

'Up by the ruins. The goat kicked it into the stream. It was under the ground.'

'My goat,' Luigi muttered. 'And my ground.' This was a considerable liberty. It was communal ground. He just wanted to get his hand on the marble. As a practised antique-forger he knew the authentic article from the bad. It could be worth a lot of money. 'And you were employed on my time.' He thought he had made out a good case for possession. He reached out for the head. 'It belongs to me.'

Caesar felt his belly tighten. He wouldn't have handed it over to God.

'How can it be? I found it.'

'Finding isn't keeping. Don't argue. I know the law.'

Caesar said stubbornly, 'It is mine.'

'You have no right to anything. You are nothing but a penniless unprivileged——' Luigi stopped short of the words 'young bastard'. 'Give it to me.'

Caesar clutched it to his chest. He retreated guardedly. 'No,' he said.

Luigi began to shout. He accompanied it with the usual theatrical gestures. One finger crooked to heaven, calling on God to witness: one finger stabbing at the boy. He acted out the majesty of justice. 'I have just told you the law.'

'I don't know anything about the law.'

'Then will you listen?'

'This is me. Look. There is my name on it: Caesar. It has waited hundreds of years up there for me to find it.'

The argument momentarily stunned Luigi. 'Are you mad? He was a great historic figure.'

'I shall be one, too.'

'You *are* mad. Hand it over,' Luigi said.

And there in the courtroom – acting it out for the audience – he demonstrated his outrage and his despair all over again.

The magistrate said faintly, 'You are wearing me out.' It was the heat that was wearing him out. The air was leaden. Molten. The sweat prickled on his skin. He had just felt the second of those fuzzy sensations. There was a carafe of water on the bench and the glass suspended on it rattled lightly as if he had nudged it with his elbow. He had done no such thing. He said to himself: stop it. You are talking yourself into a panic. It's all imagination. He was staring at the wall over Luigi's head. He saw a jagged hair-crack slip silently down it. That wasn't imagination. And the magistrate's stomach gripped. The boy had seen it, too. He stared thoughtfully at the wall. He is too young to be frightened, the magistrate thought. Well, I am an old man and I *am* frightened.

But to get on with the case.

He said to the boy, 'Go on.'

But Luigi wouldn't let him go on. He was wound up like a frustrated tragedian. He held up the flats of his hands like a traffic policeman and cried, 'As heaven is my witness . . .'

'Yes, yes,' the magistrate said impatiently. He will act me out of my mind. 'What did you do?'

'I claimed my property.'

'How?'

Luigi's index finger quivered like a school-master's cane and the wrists went all liquid. He was using his elbows now. They mesmerized the court. 'I reprimanded him . . .'

'*How?*'

'I gave him a light push.' And Luigi made a little feathery dab at the air, as if he were patting butter, to show how light a push it was. Caesar's mouth turned down at the corners. He touched his ear instinctively. More like a good cuff over the head, the magistrate thought. 'I took the marble from him. And *then* . . .' Luigi mustered all the dramatic effects. He clutched his belly. His eyes distended. He looked as if he were in the last stages of pregnancy. 'He came at me like a bullet,' he said. 'Here.' He caressed his navel. 'He butted me with his head. Like a mad bull. I fell. I struck my skull.' The hands fluttered agonizingly up to the plaster on his brow. 'He seized the marble and ran.'

'Did you?' the magistrate asked the boy.

'Yes.'

'Butt him?'

'Of course. He has a fat belly. It didn't hurt me.'

'It hurt him.'

'I intended it to. He stole my head.'

'It was an act of violence.'

'I am twelve. I have nobody. I shall not survive without a little occasional violence,' Caesar said.

And then – nothing could have been more dramatic – the bench twitched. The animal down there was getting restless. And the whole court grew rigid. There was a soft solitary boom outside. The church bell had rung by itself.

The magistrate said to the priest, 'Is there anybody in . . .?'

'The church is empty.' The priest was staring at the boy. 'God is angry.'

I am getting angry, too, the magistrate thought. You would think God had enough to do without going in for all this cheap theatre to show a twelve-year-old boy that He is annoyed.

'He is a pagan,' the priest said.

We are all pagans. Nothing has changed here since the Roman legions marched, the magistrate thought.

He was soaked with sweat. 'It is too hot to continue. The case is remanded until tomorrow.' He didn't know that

tomorrow he would be dead. The priest, too. He saw the
boy staring intensely at the marble. 'I will look after this
until then,' he said, and went into the chamber behind the
court which was his bedroom for the night.

He washed. He couldn't get the boy's yearning eyes out
of his mind. He looked at the marble. The tranquil powerful
face looked back. One Caesar is enough for this world, he
thought. And he happened to glance at the window. The
boy was outside. He was peering through the glass. His lips
moved. He seemed to be saying: take care of it. That is my
head you have there. My actual living head. They stared at
each other sympathetically for a few moments. And then
the boy went away.

II

CAESAR ambled about the square. He had time on his hands. He was no longer in employment. The villagers avoided him. They regarded him as *malefico*, meaning ill-starred. I suppose it's because I am a pagan, he thought. It didn't worry him. His namesake-hero had also been a pagan. And look what he had achieved without the patronage of God.

He was also homeless. Luigi had shouted at him, 'Get out,' and had thrown his things out of the shed. He had managed revengefully to tread on the pictures. Caesar looked at the broken glass and the mice-nibbled blankets and the rusty stove and the canvas mattress that leaked straw. It didn't seem much to accumulate in a fifth of a lifetime. It didn't worry him, either. He was twelve years of age, when life looks as if it will go on for ever. He had read somewhere that the world is a man's oyster.

Mine will be a very succulent one, he thought.

It was still oven-hot. The sky had that brazen lustre. Everything so quiet: as if waiting, waiting. The square was crowded with villagers, staring curiously at the church. Pieces of dislodged plaster lay on the cobbles. Caesar wondered what had made the bell ring.

The priest was among the crowd. He caught sight of Caesar and stared at him burningly. He crossed himself. Caesar crossed himself politely, too. He thought it was a nice gesture, though without meaning.

The villagers moved away from him *en bloc*.

It was then that he heard the steamy blare of music. It

seemed to come from just beyond the square. He went round to investigate. He grinned. Now this is something. The children had collected in a mob about a little travelling fair. There was a ramshackle old merry-go-round, a thing of bobbing horses and unicorns and other mythical beasts. They were all scabbed with peeling paint. But they looked wonderful in the sun. Some kind of panting engine drove it. It also worked the bleating calliope, which was a concoction of organ pipes that sounded better than the ones in the church. A small calm girl was collecting money from the children riding it. The owner of the fair was an ill-tempered man who was trying to rouse a somnolent beast in a cage.

Caesar had never seen a living tiger. He saw one now.

It was old and its life didn't seem very happy. Its striped skin had lost its sheen. The fair-owner was poking a whip between the bars of the cage, shouting, 'Hup, hup, Lucrezia,' and the tiger went through the weary motions of bounding and rolling and baring its teeth. They were stumps. Its ribs showed. It growled, and then its growl dwindled into a yawn. It just wanted to sleep in the sunshine. 'Hup, hup,' roared the man and the tiger hupped and tried to make a frightening sound.

It didn't frighten Caesar.

He looked at the girl. She looked back.

He went nearer to her. He said courteously, 'That is a tiger?'

'Of course.'

'Man-eating?'

She chuckled. 'She hasn't eaten a man for a great many years.'

'He is a *she*?' Caesar thought of a tiger, which should be ferocious and virile, only as a he.

'There have to be lady tigers,' the girl said. 'Or there would not be any . . .' and her voice trailed off significantly.

15

Naturally Caesar knew a little about the facts of life. He nodded.

And he gazed at the next cage. There were two apes in it. They had intelligent eyes. He was drawn fascinatedly across. He said to them softly through the bars, 'Say something to me.' And the brown mournful eyes looked back. The straw of the cage stank. Banana skins littered the floor. The girl had come behind him.

She said, 'They are chimpanzees.'

'Yes,' Caesar said wisely. He had never heard of a chimpanzee before. They looked rather like hairy, long-armed, bow-legged acrobats. They leaned against each other intimately.

'Men?' he asked.

'One man. One lady.'

'The wife?'

The question became a little superfluous, for the chimpanzees engaged lazily in a physical act. The children watching gasped. Sex is a thing of wonderment to children.

The fair-owner was now putting a pair of grey donkeys through their turn. This *was* clever. Caesar had looked after farm donkeys and had always thought them obtuse. These flashed, like quicksilver, and they spun about on little delicate hooves. Caesar thought it a miracle of virtuosity. 'Holy God,' he said. He whistled excitedly through his teeth.

'They are our dancing donkeys,' the girl said.

'I have never seen donkeys dance.'

'I trained them.'

'I congratulate you on your skill,' he said.

'Thank you. Their names are Castor and Pollux.'

'Yes.' He remembered to ask politely, 'What is your name?'

'Maria.'

'Mine is Caesar.'

'He was a great one.'

'Yes,' he said carelessly. 'I have his head somewhere.'
He didn't tell her that it was in the custody of a court.

The fair-owner yelled at Maria, 'Get back to your place.'
Children were nipping without payment on the merry-go-
round. Maria said in a low voice to Caesar, 'If you would
care for a little ride on the . . . ?'

'I have no money.'

'I am not looking,' she said demurely, turning away her
head.

Caesar waited for the opportunity. The fair-owner
smacked the dancing donkeys and they began a stately
minuet. As stately as donkeys could make it. Caesar slipped
on the back of a painted mustang and spurred it with his
heels. It reared, it bobbed, and circled the panting calliope.
Round and round he went, while the pipes blatted out a
steamy version of Verdi's *La Donna è Mobile*. Verdi would
not have recognized it. Caesar suddenly felt a hard coarse
hand on his neck. The fair-owner said, 'I saw you. You
young bastard.' The description was accurate, but painful.
He began to shake Caesar. 'Pay up.'

'I would. If I had the money.'

'Father,' Maria said . . .

'You, too. Shut up. This is not a free church-picnic. You
will run me into bankruptcy.'

He threw Caesar into the dirt. While he lay there he
exacted payment by kicking him in the ribs. The donkeys
stopped dancing. They watched Caesar sympathetically.
The two mournful chimpanzees sighed. The tiger was too
old to feel emotion. It rolled over and went to sleep.

Caesar rubbed his ribs. They hurt. He felt his pride and
his dignity ooze away from him like water through a holed
bucket. He looked at the fair-owner's belly. It was as pendu-
lous as Luigi's. And as inviting. One good butt, he thought,
to teach him . . . Then he caught sight of Maria's face. He

17

checked himself. He said coldly, 'It was nothing to do with her. I did it while she wasn't looking.'

She coloured with gratitude.

He rose, dusting himself down elaborately, and went.

He idled the afternoon away up by the ruins. Something else important might be there. He found nothing but bits of mosaic, a scrap or two of pottery, and a coin that was so bent and discoloured that he threw it away. The head on it was bearded. It wasn't the great Caesar's. He went back, passing the cows in the fields. He said to them, 'What is the matter? Have you lost your tongues?' They were too listless even to graze. The nervous bovine eyes rolled. He stared at the birds, lined like expectant buzzards along the branches of the trees. Silence. 'Sing,' he said to them. 'Why are you all frightened?' Not even a flutter of wings. Something was very wrong.

He looked up at the sky. The sun was sinking. A great bronze radiance burned on the horizon. Heat came down from it. He felt the sods underneath him roll. The birds fluttered off and the air was black with their myriads. Caesar pressed the grass. It seemed reasonably solid. One by one the silent birds came back.

At dusk he returned to the fair. He could hear the wheezy music at a distance. It glittered with festoons of fairy lights. It was crowded now. He felt less conspicuous as he stood and watched the donkeys dance, the tiger snarl unconvincingly and do a roll through a hoop. The effort seemed to hurt every aching muscle. The chimpanzees did a smart balancing act on chairs. It delighted everybody but the chimpanzees. They seemed sad. They are probably hungry, Caesar thought. He looked at the fair-owner's surly face. I should have thudded his belly. And the merry-go-round whirled and the thick strains of Verdi and Puccini panted into the night.

Caesar saw Maria by the pay-desk. She saw him. She

seemed expectant. Her face warmed instantly. He nodded. She looked at her father, then nodded back. He came across.

'Did he hit you?' he asked.

'No.'

He had. She put her discoloured wrist behind her. Caesar pretended not to notice.

'I do not admire him,' he said.

'He is still my father.'

'I don't have one.'

'Everybody has a . . .' then the significance of what he had said penetrated. She looked at him curiously. 'I am sorry to hear that.'

'I am a bastard.' He might as well come out with it frankly. It was only a kind of stamp, after all, like the bar sinister on a knight's shield.

'You are innocent of it,' she said. 'It wasn't anything you did . . .'

'There isn't anything to be innocent about. Or guilty, either. It isn't a crime. There was some soldier. *Inglesi*. I have his fair hair. He made me in my mother.' It was the literal truth. 'He didn't wait to see if the result was satisfactory.' Caesar's father, a brawling Northumbrian miner, would have been astonished to know that there had been a result. He wouldn't have cared. He had a whole legitimate brood to take care of. 'My mother didn't wait long, either. She died,' Caesar said.

'That is sad.'

'I do not miss them.'

'That is why it is sad.' Maria heaved a sigh. She looked at the lank ashen hair, which was the mark of his great difference. He isn't really Italian at all. He is rather exciting. She looked at his torn pants, feeling a warm desire to repair them. The maternal instinct begins early with Italian girls. 'It is not good to be so alone,' she said.

'Everybody is alone inside himself. I need nobody. What

I have to do in this world I will do. And I will do it by myself.'

Maria caught her breath. She felt a great thrill.

'If your father beats you,' Caesar told her coolly, 'wait until he is asleep, then beat him back. One has to preserve one's dignity.'

Maria shivered. She wouldn't have dreamed of it. It would have meant a kind of guerrilla warfare, for her father beat her every day.

'How hot it is,' she said. He *is* exciting. She dabbed her face.

'Something is going to happen.'

'You think so?'

'The sky is going to fall in.'

'What? How do you know?'

'I have been watching it.' The conversation was getting to be a little difficult, for children were pushing by the pay-desk to mount the merry-go-round. 'Don't worry. I shall be somewhere at hand.'

Luigi's family suddenly arrived.

Caesar drew back. Luigi glared at him. He didn't say anything. But he couldn't stop his emotional hands working on their own. The fingers said to Caesar: you are a monster. The liquid wrists described the circumstances of his birth. The elbows made another insult.

Luigi's wife said to him, 'Assassin. You will kill somebody in the end.'

You, I hope, Caesar thought.

'They will put you away for ever,' the daughter Sophia cried. Caesar, who knew all about the anatomy of birth, wondered how the simple act of love could produce an ill-favoured specimen like that.

The family mounted the merry-go-round. Maria left the desk to start it. Caesar watched her release the lever that let in the clutch: watched her speed it up with the throttle. He had a good eye for engines. The lights flickered. The pipes wheezed unmelodiously. One of them always missed fire, giving the music a kind of hiccuping beat.

Each time Luigi whirled by Caesar his fingers made another insult. Luigi's wife glowered at him. Sophia waggled her thumbs in her ears and put out her tongue at him and laughed.

Caesar remembered the horror of the dark, rat-ridden shed. The exorbitant rent. He began to catalogue the history of petty cruelties. He rubbed his ear: the one that had been slapped. *One has to preserve one's dignity*, he thought. Maria watched him with compassion in her heart. He moved off. She lost him in the crowd. She wondered if she would ever see him again. The fair, which was about as static as a flea, never stayed more than one night in a village – tomorrow the mules would be hitched to the cages and they would be off. She hardly noticed the increased quiver and racket of the merry-go-round.

The elated screeches of the children roused her. It was going faster and faster. '*Faster, faster,*' the children cried. It whirled as if it would burst into orbit. The painted beasts bucked like unbroken bronchos. Luigi, astride a unicorn, clutched the horns desperately. His eyes rolled with terror. He was too fat to hold his seat. His wife was as stiff as a board. Her backside hammered on her mount's rump. Sophia screamed.

Maria wondered why the engine should run away with itself. She saw Caesar with his hand on the throttle. And understood.

Everything that happened then was bedlam. The rim of the buckboard tilted: the merry-go-round scraped earth. It split. The music gasped off. Only Sophia's screams could be heard. Luigi fell into the dirt. Maria saw her father fall thunderously on Caesar.

The magistrate had decided to go early to bed. It had

been a long ride through the mountains. He didn't expect, anyway, to sleep through the oppressive heat. He heard the policeman calling through the door. He opened it. The corridor was crowded. He saw Luigi holding his face. There was a little blood on it. He was too overwrought to open his mouth. It didn't matter: his fingers could speak. His wife was dishevelled; looking into her frozen shocked eyes the magistrate thought she was mad. Sophia snivelled. There was an enraged black-browed man trying to get at Caesar. The policeman held him. Only he was calm.

When he had heard everything, the magistrate said to the policeman, 'Leave him here with me. Wait outside.'

'In case of violence . . .'

'He will not attack me. The rest can go.'

The fair-owner – the black-browed man – said in a stifled voice, 'I will kill him.'

The magistrate said coldly, 'You will kill nobody but your donkeys. I have seen you at it in other villages.'

He said to Caesar, 'Sit,' when they were alone.

Then, in a gentler voice:

'Why did you do it?'

'One has to preserve one's dignity,' Caesar said.

'You mean your pride.'

'I am proud, too,' Caesar said.

'Did nobody ever tell you that pride goeth before a fall?'

'I have fallen a few times.' Caesar shrugged. 'I have always managed to pick myself up.'

'Not this time,' the magistrate said dryly. 'You have done a lot of damage.'

'I am sorry. I didn't intend it. I wish I could make it good. I only earn enough to eat.'

'I remanded you on the surety of your good behaviour. Do you know what that means?'

'Vaguely.'

'You could go off and do some more damage. I am afraid I will have to keep you in custody for the night.'

'It's all right. The prison cell will suit me. I have nowhere to sleep, anyway,' Caesar said.

'That's what I thought,' the magistrate said with relief. He was glad to seize on the excuse. He hated to lock a boy in a cell for the night. 'Have you had supper?'

'No.'

'I haven't eaten mine. It's so stifling.' There was some sausage and bread and a carafe of flat wine. 'Take it.'

Caesar ate silently, wolfishly. He didn't take his eyes off the marble on the table.

The magistrate followed his glance over to the imperious head. 'He changed the whole world,' he said softly. 'Things were never the same after he lived.'

'That's what I like about him,' Caesar said. 'No half measures. We do the thing properly or not at all.'

'We.' The magistrate twinkled. Only the best family connections. Nobody is ever going to accuse this boy of humility. He waited until Caesar had polished off the last crumb, then called in the policeman, who took him away.

The magistrate composed himself for sleep. It avoided him for a long time. The air had the taste and smell of a bad bakery. As he finally drifted off he thought, I wish I were young again. There is someone who reaches out for life with both hands. He couldn't get the boy's resolute face out of his mind.

It was the last face he ever saw: the last thought he ever had.

At one in the morning the whole mountainous spine of Italy split in half. The major cleft ran clear through the region of Abruzzi. The village of Lorenzo of the Angels was situated exactly on the line of the fault. The shock was felt as far away as Japan. It began with a soft rumble, as if night thunder were reverberating in the hills. Then the mountains rattled as if a dog were shaking them like a rat in its teeth. The foundations of the earth cracked. There was a terrible roaring. In less than three seconds the death toll in the villages of central Italy was uncountable. People ran out into the streets of Rome and Naples. Almost nobody ran out into the streets of those lonely townlets up in the hills.

The earthquake was repeated half an hour later, but it was like vengeful bombers returning to a target already almost completely destroyed. The magistrate lay under rubble. The town-hall was the strongest building in the village, and when it split, half of it stood raggedly: the rest of it fell. The magistrate was in the part that fell. Caesar, sleeping in the cell, was in the part that stood.

A few dogs went yapping madly through the dust-filled streets. There was a little whimpering from under the stricken houses. Then silence. There was a bright moon. The twittering birds finally descended. A breeze stirred and started to blow the dust away.

III

MAJOR-GENERAL BRAZZOLO sat on the tailboard of one of his supply-trucks, peering desolately at what was left of the village of Lorenzo of the Angels. For ten hours it had been the nerve-centre of his rescue operation. There hadn't been much he could rescue. The square was heaped with dislodged masonry. Dust hung in the air, and permeating the dust was the stench of death. He had recovered some dozens of bodies, but only God – who kept an accurate record of humanity – knew how many still lay under the rubble of the collapsed houses.

It distressed the major-general terribly. He was a highly emotional man. Although he was a soldier he wasn't familiar with death.

He had a burial party digging trenches. He had the few survivors in one of his trucks. A whole frantic family named Pirelli. The man, Luigi, who said he was an antique dealer, had to be restrained from clawing his way into his squashed shop. His wife stood blaming God. She was a fury. She looked mad. The daughter, Sophia, just wept.

And there was a small calm girl who was left with a perambulating fair. The father was dead. He lay under the ruins of a merry-go-round. God, in His strange mercy, had preserved the animals. The two mules that drew the cages: a pair of donkeys that pranced mechanically in the sun: two sad apes: and a worn-out old tiger that was scarcely worth turning into a rug.

'Hurry,' the major-general called out to Lieutenant Arnolfo, his aide.

The lieutenant said patiently, 'Yes, major-general.' He was a pleasant olive-skinned young man. 'We are just filling up the trenches. We will not be long.'

The sun blazed. 'This place will soon be pestilential.' The major-general mopped his face. He just wanted to get away.

He had arrived quite by accident in the village. The earthquake had caught him up in the mountains with a detachment of forty-four men and nine tank-transports. He had been carrying out tests with low-level projectiles. He wasn't really a soldier; he was a desk-technician; a rocketry expert with the brass of a high-ranking officer on his sleeve. It had been a frightful night. He had seen a whole valley split like a rotten apple. He wasn't very devout, but it could have turned him into a religious man. He had lost a tank-transport in the first shock, and two trucks in the second. He hadn't lost a man. He was a sea-lover. He was based in Naples. He had always disliked mountains. After that night of horror he disliked them even more.

He had heard disjointed reports of the national disaster on his radio. He came down into Lorenzo of the Angels and saw what such a disaster was like. He could hardly get his remaining eight tank-transports and his supply-trucks into the square. The village had been shaken flat. He could hear terrified cows lowing. The buzzards were busy with the dead.

And he stared at it all, his soft wet mouth pursed like a button, shaking his head. '*Mama mia*,' he murmured to himself. It wasn't a soldier's remark, but Neapolitans, in moments of pure shock, always said, '*Mama mia*'.

He sometimes wished he could look like a soldier. He practised martial poses in front of a mirror. It was no good. He was the wrong shape. He was a very fat man. His whole face worked when he shouted an order. He was given to fits of rage, although he was really very good-hearted. The uniform and the fat clown inside it were always in conflict. It turned him into a choleric man.

He heard somebody shout. It was Sergeant Segni: the men called him *Naso* because of his long nose. He was lying in the dust on his belly, trying to peer through a low grating. Lieutenant Arnolfo ran across. The major-general thought impatiently: we will never get away. He went over to join them.

Sergeant Naso looked up and said wonderingly, 'There is a boy down there.'

'There can't be.'

'I can see him.'

'Let me look.'

And the major-general lowered himself gingerly to the ground. He stared through the bars. It was as dark as a dungeon. It was exactly what it had once been. It was an ancient building. The inside was hazy with dust. A lot of rubble must have collapsed.

'I can't see anything,' he said to Lieutenant Arnolfo. 'What is this place?'

'The prison, I think.'

'The *what*?'

'It's the town-hall.'

'What is a boy doing in prison?' The boy answered the question himself. The major-general found himself staring into a grey-eyed young face with very fair hair. The boy had swarmed up a wooden bench propped against the grating.

'It's a long story,' he said. 'Can we go into it later? I just want to get out.'

'How long have you been there?'

'All night.'

'Is there a door?'

'It's locked.' Prison doors are usually locked.

'Wait.' As the major-general got up it occurred to him

27

that a cell with a locked door is a place in which one can only wait. He felt annoyed with himself.

Lieutenant Arnolfo was feeling the thickness of the bars. 'We can cut them out in an hour.'

The major-general said irascibly, 'The whole place is dangerous. We have to get away. He had no right to be there.'

'We have to get him out.'

'I know that,' the major-general shouted. 'All I said was that he had no right to be there.'

And his soft rosebud of a mouth gasped. He had just felt another tremor. He squinted up at the church. It was tilted at an insane angle. The bell, jammed in the belfry, stuck out like the fruit of some giant pod. The church didn't so much fall, as wilt. It disappeared into a broken stump under a smoking heap of debris. The major-general now had seven tank-transports. One of them had been parked by it. Thank God, nobody had been in it.

'Hurry,' he said thickly to the sergeant.

One of the transport-fitters got busy with a hack-saw. There was only room for one to operate. The boy had vanished. Sergeant Naso squatted by the grating and called in.

'You there, boy?'

'Where would I be?' came the hollow reply.

Sergeant Naso chuckled. 'How is it down there?'

'Uncomfortable.'

'Give us an hour.'

'And if I don't?'

The sergeant chuckled again. 'What is your name?'

'Caesar.'

'A great name. Be like him.'

Now it was the boy's turn to chuckle. Both stopped chuckling as the ground heaved like a loose mattress. The sergeant heard the clatter of falling rubble in the dark cell and grew nervous. He heard the boy choke and cough and knew that he was all right.

Dust oozed through the grating. The soldier with the hack-saw tore frenziedly into the bar. It seemed as thick as his wrist. The sun glimmered foggily into the cell. Most of the ceiling had fallen with last night's shock – the rest fell now. Caesar clambered over lath and reeking plaster, wrapping his handkerchief about his mouth. He thought: next time it won't be plaster, it'll be the whole roof. They'll be all day at those bars. He didn't think he had all day. He looked at the great oak door. The stone lintel was slipping. The wood was distorted. If I can find something to lever it, he thought. He had the bench. He dragged it over the rubble and inserted the edge. He shoved. The lock was bent out of its jamb. He wrenched it away. The door wouldn't budge for the rubble. He dug it clear and shoved again. He could just slip like an eel through the crack. He had hardly done so when the lintel crashed down the door and the stones of the roof fell in.

The soldier cutting at the grating shrank from it as if it were not worth going on. Sergeant Naso bit his knuckles with distress. Lieutenant Arnolfo sighed.

Caesar went along the littered passage, and on upstairs. A door flapped open. He looked in. He recognized the magistrate's bed-chamber. The bed was under rubble. He saw a thin pale hand dangling out of the mess. He wasn't a bad man – he was kind to me, he thought. He was looking for something else. He saw it miraculously untouched on the table.

He wrapped the marble head in his shirt. He followed the stream of light along the wrecked corridor. He came out into the sunshine at the back of the town-hall.

There was nothing recognizable left of the village. Huge vehicles bearing tanks with long snout-like guns were parked about the devastated square. He wondered where

29

they had come from. A detachment of soldiers was filling a trench. They hardly glanced at him. He went on round and saw a grizzled sergeant poking a flash-light through the grating. A fat officer with much brass lay on his belly, trying to pierce the murk. Another officer, a junior with a gentle olive face, watched them, too.

'It's all right. You needn't bother,' he said.

The fat officer with the brass looked up at him impatiently. He said, 'Go away.' Then the fair hair and the grey eyes registered. He looked at him again. His face was inflamed with blood from lying on his belly. His voice was congested. 'How did you get here?'

'I walked out.'

The sergeant suppressed a sigh and a chuckle. 'Boy, you gave us a bad ten minutes,' he said.

Lieutenant Arnolfo watched his superior. He knew his choleric temper. The major-general picked himself up. He had lost dignity, lying in the dirt. 'Where have you been?' he said to Caesar.

'I had something to collect.'

The major-general wiped his face. It was filthy. 'Get into the truck with the others,' he said.

Caesar looked at the survivors in the truck. He saw the Pirelli family.

'Why?'

'We are leaving.'

'Where are you going?'

The major-general wasn't used to being interrogated. 'Naples.'

'Thank you. I am going to Rome,' Caesar said.

The major-general glared at him. 'You will go where you are told.'

This is a curiously excitable man, Caesar thought. He is too fat for a soldier. He looks more like a shopkeeper.

'Not necessarily.'

'Did you hear what I said?'

'I think everybody must have heard. I am going to Rome. That is where my destiny lies,' Caesar said.

The major-general was aware that his men had stopped filling in the trench to listen. He took off his ornamental cap. Like most 'scientific' officers he was insanely conscious of his importance. He was losing face, minute by minute. 'You will go to Naples.'

Caesar began suddenly to dislike him. He looked at his round belly. He was tempted to butt it.

'Do not argue with the major-general,' Lieutenant Arnolfo said to him softly. He liked the look of the boy. This is an independent young mind.

'I am not in his army. I am my own master. And Rome is where I am going,' Caesar said.

The major-general flushed. Apart from his fits of rage, which came from his inner insecurity, he was a kindly man. He was a good father. He liked children. But he was being made to look small. He said irritably to Sergeant Naso, 'Throw him into the truck.'

The sergeant sighed. He was one of those grizzled old sweats who hold armies together. He disliked the order. He approached reluctantly.

'Boy, do not give me trouble.'

'I hope I shall not have to.' Caesar backed away.

He couldn't back very far. He was almost up against a truck. He looked round. His eyes explored the situation. The soldier who had been sawing at the bars had left his carbine on the tailboard.

'Settle for Naples. You could have quite a destiny there,' Sergeant Naso said.

'Rome.'

'Throw him into the truck,' the major-general repeated.

Caesar reached for the carbine.

'Throw me,' he said.

Sergeant Naso looked at it thoughtfully. He was familiar with weapons. He saw that the safety catch was down. Lieutenant Arnolfo saw it, too. Their eyes met. They decided instinctively to say nothing.

The soldiers stared. The major-general's moon-face quivered. His eyes thickened with blood. 'Take it away from him,' he said.

'Major-general,' Sergeant Naso said. 'That rifle is pointed at my guts.' It wasn't. It was pointed at the major-general's round belly.

'I order you . . .'

'It would be a cruel and unnatural order.'

'Lieutenant Arnolfo!'

'I am thirty years of age,' Lieutenant Arnolfo said. 'Forgive me. I would like to live to be thirty-one.'

'You will do as you are told . . .'

'Major-general,' the lieutenant whispered. 'This is terrible for discipline. The men are watching.'

'I cannot let him defy me.'

'He is not important. What does he matter? He is just a boy. Let him go.'

'Yes,' the major-general said. 'He is not important.' But he was still trembling. 'Let him go. To the devil, no doubt.' He came to terms with an ugly situation. He glared at the men, who bent quickly over their mattocks. He stared furiously at Caesar and went off to sit in his staff-car.

'Give it to me,' the sergeant said to Caesar. 'That is a dangerous weapon.'

'It's all right. The safety catch is down.'

'You knew?'

'Naturally.'

The sergeant's eyes narrowed. 'You will try that once too often.'

'Not if I am careful,' Caesar said.

Sergeant Naso grinned. 'You know how far it is to Rome?'

'I will walk it if necessary.'

'You will, too. Good walking,' the sergeant said.

Caesar slung his shirt bearing the marble head over his shoulder like a knapsack. He walked round the back of the square.

He expected to find nothing of the fair. He found Maria sitting on the splintered step of the merry-go-round. The calliope was all twisted pipes. They were finished with Puccini and Verdi. The caravan was mashed. The mules stood, though. Mules will live through anything. And the two cages were intact. The aged tiger, Lucrezia, slept in one. It had hardly been disturbed by the earthquake. The apes sat disconsolately in the other. The donkeys fidgeted mechanically in the sun. They only wanted to dance.

'Where is your father?' Caesar asked Maria.

She looked up to heaven. She spread her hands.

'Do not worry. I never had a father. You can do without them,' Caesar said.

He looked the mules over. He felt the fetlocks. He knew mules. An idea was forming in his mind.

'You cannot sit here,' he said.

'The officer says that I must leave them behind.' Her eyes filled with tears. 'He has no room for the cages. And the animals will only hold him up, he said.'

'Which officer?'

'The fat one. With the gold on his hat.'

'You do not have to take any notice of him. I have just ignored him,' Caesar said. He thought: it *is* a long way to Rome. It will be quicker with mules. And he thought rather calculatingly: it is worth taking her along. 'I am going to Rome. Do you wish to come with me?'

'All of us?'

Caesar only wanted the mules. He had no option. He shrugged. 'Of course,' he said.

'Do you know how *far* it is to Rome?'

33

'I am not frightened.'

'You are sure?'

'That I know how far it is to Rome?'

'That you are not frightened.'

'Fear is a habit. Habits can be conquered. Do you wish to join me?'

She looked at him. She had that maternal feeling again. She thought: I will mend that tear in his pants. I have never seen such fair hair. He is twice as stimulating as Chianti. 'Yes. Of course,' she said.

'Is there food?'

'A loaf in the caravan. Some meat.'

'Leave everything to me. Just sit still.'

He tore aside the smashed planks. He found the food-safe. The loaf was stale. He had eaten worse. He wrapped it up. The meat was clouded with humming ravenous flies. He smelled it. He wasn't over-critical where food was concerned. He left it to the flies. During the excavation he found some rope. We may need it, he thought. He found seat cushions and set them on the roof of the leading cage. The other cage was fixed to trail behind it. He hitched up the mules. He tied the two donkeys to the rear. He remembered their names. Castor and Pollux. The apes were anonymous. I will call them Number One and Number Two, he thought. He rummaged on in the caravan's guts. He found a lamp and a crowbar. They may come in useful. Most important of all he found a shotgun and a case of shells. It filled him with pleasure. We will not starve. Not as long as there are rabbits in the ditches and fowl in the sky.

He climbed up on to the cushions on the leading cage. He beckoned down to Maria.

'Get up.'

'Yes,' she said meekly. She had no will but his.

Caesar flicked the reins. The mules looked round. They seemed not to recognize their new master. He said some-

34

thing explicit to them. He kicked the nearest rump. They heaved. The cortège moved into the square.

It reeked of diesel oil: throbbed with the roar of the tank-transports. The army convoy was forming up for departure. The fearsome guns wheeled, one by one, into line. Caesar trotted by. The donkeys' heels frisked. They were happy. Numbers One and Two chattered. Lucrezia slept. Sergeant Naso, staring down at the cages from his truck, said wonderingly to Lieutenant Arnolfo, 'Holy God. I don't believe it.'

Lieutenant Arnolfo thought: life at that age is one vast adventure. It is wonderful. Look at the sun on the boy's face. I wish I were young again.

Major-General Brazzolo, watching from his staff-car with a glazed look in his eyes, thought: somebody should warn the girl. That young demon will lead her into danger. They will die on the way.

The cages disappeared round the bend of the road. They entered the defile that led into the mountains.

The major-general was in a terrible haste to get away. The mere sight of the flattened village, with its unretrieved dead, shocked him. It took half an hour to form up the unwieldy convoy. He finally waved from his staff-car. They got under way.

The road was hardly more than a twisting thread. The rocky slopes, rearing up from the verge, echoed the roar of the tank-transports. They were still nowhere near the great peaks. They made good time. They rumbled on. They rounded a curve and ground down almost to a crawl. The cages rattled ahead.

Mules have no sense of urgency. With them it is always *mañana*: tomorrow is also a day. The convoy belched behind at a walking pace. The major-general could see the boy's fair hair over the roof of the leading cage. He sounded the horn. The boy didn't even turn his head. This is ludicrous. You are keeping the army waiting, the major-general thought. He had almost no sense of humour. The situation became insufferable. Again he sounded the horn. It had no noticeable effect on the mules. He said impatiently to his driver, 'We have to get by.'

The driver looked at him with surprise. Short of taking off, he didn't see how. The road was barely wide enough for the tank-transports.

The major-general looked back. He could see heads peering out of every cab. In some strange way the whole iron weight of the convoy seemed to be shoving him on. He couldn't understand what was happening to him. He began to sweat. His military 'image' was at stake. He put his head out of the staff-car, shouting at the cages, 'Get out of the way.' The horn blared and blared.

The boy didn't look round.

The major-general went a little mad. He felt that his men were watching him critically. They weren't. They were in no hurry. Soldiers are never in a hurry. They merely wondered what was griping their major-general. The slopes resounded with the horn like a shooting gallery. 'Get out of the way,' they heard him shouting at the cages. 'Get out of the way.'

The driver thought: he must be in a great hurry to get back to his desk.

Sergeant Naso thought – in crude Italian idiom – this paper general of ours will blow his nut.

He demeans the army, Lieutenant Arnolfo thought with disgust.

The major-general suddenly contained himself. I am making a spectacle of myself, he thought. He wiped his face. A small vein thudded like a frustrated animal in his neck. I will give myself apoplexy for nothing. The convoy crawled on, clanking ponderously. At long, long last they came to the fork.

The left-hand prong wound desolately on through the valley towards Tetragoni. This was the road to Rome. The mules plodded along it. The right-hand prong went straight on up to meet the main highway to Naples. This was the road the convoy took. As it gathered thunderous speed, clanking up into the mountains, the major-general looked down at the cages out of the corner of his eye.

He took the apes as a personal affront. The donkeys skipped. The tiger slept. The girl gazed ahead with dignity. The sun glinted on the fair hair as the boy looked up. Thank God, the major-general thought, as the cages grew smaller and smaller, vanishing into the solitude of the forests, I have seen the last of him.

He had never been more wrong in his life.

IV

SOME distant eye – God's, for instance – watching the ruined spine of Italy, might have seen Major-General Brazzolo's unit and the cages go their separate ways. The tank-transports thudded powerfully up into the mountains. There wasn't much to hinder them. They expected to reach the Naples highway by dusk. The diesels sang. Then, round about mid-afternoon, with the sun blazing down on smashed silent·ravines, they stopped singing. They began to meet avalanches. The earthquake had loosened whole rock formations. The convoy stopped and the men poured out of the trucks to clear the road.

This was repeated every half hour. Then every fifteen minutes. The road was blocked by bigger and bigger boulders. The men began to curse.

Sergeant Naso directed them, barking ferociously. Like all grizzled army sweats, he didn't dirty his hands. Lieutenant Arnolfo, being a democrat, split his nails shifting boulders with the men. The sergeant thought they should have taken the road down into the valley, turning off later for Naples. Like Caesar, he visualized the crust of the earth as a cracked overbaked loaf. The higher they went, the wider the cracks. He said to Lieutenant Arnolfo, as they descended for the sixth time, 'This is a bad joke.'

'I don't see you laughing,' Lieutenant Arnolfo said. 'I don't see you shifting stones, either.'

'We should have stayed below.'

'Tell the major-general.'

'I did. We don't use the same language. He talks in

logarithms. He can't open his mouth without a slide-rule in his hand.'

'So?'

'He told me not to argue with a high-ranking officer.' Sergeant Naso looked wisely down his big nose. He knew that N.C.O.s were the cement that kept an army together. 'I shall ignore him.'

Lieutenant Arnolfo looked at his bleeding hands. 'Will you do me a favour?'

'If I can.'

Lieutenant Arnolfo put his shoulder against a boulder. 'Ignore me, too,' he said.

Down in the valley the cages rattled. Clop, clop, went the mules. They hadn't changed the rhythm of their pace. The birds sang from the tall dark trees. The forest loomed like a thick primeval curtain over the road. Caesar sat on the roof of the leading cage, Maria at his side. He thought: she is quiet. That is good. I do not like women who talk too much. She glanced at the glinting hairs on his arms and thought: he is shy. But confident. This wilderness is terrifying. But I feel safe with him.

By midday they were deep in the silent valley. They met nobody. There was nobody to meet. They saw through the trees a distant smashed roof, a ravaged farmhouse; there was a toy-like village on the slopes that looked as if the bored child that had made it had kicked it flat.

And then, far to the right, somewhere over the soaring trees, a blotched pillar of smoke marred the hot blue sky. That is probably Tetragoni, Caesar thought. More likely, it *was* Tetragoni. He could see specks wheeling in the sky. The buzzards were busy. Maria winced. Caesar said nothing. We are alive: and life to the living is all that matters. Clop, clop, went the rhythmic mules.

And now the tortured earth began to hinder them, too. They met falls of soft rubble. The cages rode them. Then rocks littered the road, and these couldn't be ridden. Caesar shifted them. All this ate the afternoon away. The first violent quake had toppled great pines, and the second had flicked them like matchsticks across the road. Caesar had to unhitch the mules to drag them out of the way. They grumbled. Caesar understood mules. They had certain sensitive organs; Maria watched with shock as Caesar imposed his will on them.

He said to her calmly, 'Somebody has to be the master. The sooner they find out the better.'

The mules strained. They made obscene noises. 'Be as disgusting as you like. So long as you do as you are told,' Caesar said.

God's watching eye, which sees even sparrows fall, must have seen the cages crawling arduously along the valley: and the army, up in the arid heights, hardly crawling at all.

The convoy was meeting whole smashed slopes. The major-general sweated. The heat was frightful. He tried not to show his despair. The men were growing rebellious. They were more out of the trucks than in. They had never seen such terrible fissures. The diesels thudded; the unbreathable air was blue with smoke. They wouldn't meet the Naples highway at dusk. It was problematical if they would meet it at all. The road was split like the rind of a dried orange. The tank-transports crunched along it delicately.

And then they came to a gaping fissure that not even the most delicate tank-transport could cross. It was like something out of the moon-landscape. A mountain had broken in half. The men sat. The gesture had a brutal significance. Sergeant Naso's eyes narrowed. He knew that his authority had been re-asserted. Lieutenant Arnolfo sighed. He played the piano; he looked at his hands and wondered if he would ever play it again.

'Turn round,' Major-General Brazzolo said tiredly. He

hated to let Sergeant Naso have the last word. The sergeant had it.

'Back to the valley,' he said.

At about this time the cages were leaving the valley. There was a glimpse of great peaks. The road now rose to meet them. Caesar was content. They were moving. Lucrezia rolled in her cage like a retired dowager. The chimpanzees made love in the other. The donkeys pranced.

And then suddenly they came on a shattered building. Caesar guessed that it was religious; he saw a ruined spire and its cross tilted crookedly against the sky. The ancient tiled roof had fallen in. It was the Convent of the Child Jesus. As Caesar rattled nearer he saw the glimmer of two white head-dresses under the poplars. They were stained with grime. Both ladies were haggard. They were the Mother-Superior Beatrice and Sister Ursula. Both were very old. Their cheekbands were torn. They stood with a certain stricken dignity, watching the cages approach. Caesar stopped.

Mother Beatrice said to him softly, '*Buon giorno.*'

'*Buon giorno,*' he said.

V

CAESAR thought carefully: this is going to present certain difficulties. I feel it in my bones. It is going to be very hard to refuse them. There is only room for two of us.

He wasn't being heartless. He had merely developed a keen sense of survival.

He said to Mother Beatrice, whom he took to be the senior, 'There isn't much left of your building.'

She looked back at the collapsed convent. 'Not much, my son,' she said.

He saw her hands trembling. He felt only remotely sorry for her. It is hard for the young to feel sorry for the old.

The two nuns were staring intently at Lucrezia. Neither had ever seen a tiger. They had certainly never seen donkeys that skipped. With or without music, they were never quite still. Once, in the dim years of her novicehood, Mother Beatrice had seen chimpanzees in the zoo at Rome. These looked remarkably intelligent. Not to say amorous. She turned away her head.

'It's bad everywhere,' Caesar said politely.

She sighed. 'It is as providence wills.'

And if he had been by himself that would have ended the conversation. He ran his fingers over the marble head wrapped in his shirt. Imperial Caesar had no time for sentiment. He would have gone on.

He got ready to flick the reins. Maria put her hand on his. 'Wait,' she said.

Caesar thought: she is like all women. They do not know when it is fitting only for men to speak.

Mother Beatrice looked up at him curiously. Then at Maria. 'You are quite alone?'

Maria glanced at Caesar. 'We are together,' she said.

Temporarily, Caesar thought. She mustn't make too much of it. He travels fastest, who travels alone.

Mother Beatrice said with pity, 'You are far from home?'

Maria waved at the cages. 'I have never known any other home.'

'My child,' Mother Beatrice exclaimed, 'where can you be going?'

'Rome.'

It flashed through Mother Beatrice's mind: they are sent by heaven.

Caesar sensed the flash. Nothing definite had been suggested. But he began to feel slightly trapped.

There was a question trembling on Maria's tongue. She was almost too frightened to ask it. 'Where are the rest of the Sisters?'

'We are all that are left,' Sister Ursula said. She was the small one. Mother Beatrice was rather large. Sister Ursula tended to flutter. Mother Beatrice was ineffably calm. That was why one was Mother-Superior and the other the convent almoner. They were complementary. One led, the other followed. They loved each other. 'Those we found we buried. We have been at it all morning.' Sister Ursula peered at her worn fingers. They were blistered. The pale wizened face, framed by the torn cheekband, was haunted. 'The rest lie under the roof. Heaven will know where to find them.'

Tears started to Maria's eyes. 'God help them.'

'He did,' Mother Beatrice said. 'It was swift. And merciful.'

Caesar thought that it might have been even more merciful if God had not let it happen at all.

He tugged again at the reins. 'Well,' he said briskly,

'we have to be . . .' and for the second time Maria said, 'Wait.' He looked at her. She was undisciplined. He was going to have trouble with her. 'We cannot leave them,' she said.

'This is not a bus.'

'Just the same.'

'Someone will come along.'

'*We* have come along. It was fate.'

'I do not believe in fate.'

All this passed between them in whispers.

'Well, I do,' she said spiritedly. 'They are the brides of heaven.'

'Heaven should look after its brides better.'

'If you want to go, get off and walk. They are my cages,' she said.

He thought: she has a mind of her own. I will do something about it, by and by. But I am *not* going to walk. The mules waited. 'If you would care to join us,' he said courteously to the two nuns. 'I cannot promise that it will be very comfortable.'

'You are kind,' Mother Beatrice said.

'It is nothing.'

'But we cannot go without God.'

Caesar was under the curious impression that it was part of God's bargain with priests and nuns that He went with them everywhere.

'We have to take Him back to Rome,' Sister Ursula said.

Caesar wondered what she was talking about. He stared at her. Maria stared, too.

'Come,' Mother Beatrice said. She beckoned. 'Get down. Come and see.'

They climbed off the cages. They followed the two nuns through the bent gates. They picked their way over rubble. There was a plaster statue of the virgin and the child in the littered garden. It wasn't damaged, though covered with

44

dust. Caesar looked at the tranquil maternal face. Then he looked at the face of the child. 'Which is God?'

'The child. That is his mother.'

He is very young to be God, Caesar thought. He had always pictured God as having a large beard.

Mother Beatrice blew a little dust off the statue. 'It was given to our order four hundred years ago by the great Pope Julius. You remember him? He was Michelangelo's patron.' Caesar nodded gravely. He had never heard of Pope Julius. But he had heard of Michelangelo. 'It came from the Church of Santa Maria della Grazie in Rome. Its time here is over. Now it must go back to where it came from,' she said.

'Why?'

'Call it a holy duty.'

'It doesn't look very strong. It won't travel well.'

'It has survived this cataclysm.'

'Why did he make it? If he is God?'

Sister Ursula swallowed. 'You ask good questions. When you are older you will understand the answers,' she said.

'I'll tell you something I *do* understand. That is very heavy. And Rome is a long way.'

Mother Beatrice stared into the cool, critical, grey eyes. She would never have children of her own: her heart creaked slightly as she looked at this boy. 'It's a challenge, isn't it?'

'Not to me.'

'What brought you here?'

'My brain. My sense of judgment. And the mules. Though I had to kick them now and again,' he said.

'He isn't really as violent as he sounds,' Maria said to Mother Beatrice. The two women watched him humorously. 'He just likes to assert himself.'

'It is a manly virtue.'

'We will be glad to carry God back to Rome,' Maria said.

45

Caesar said in her ear, 'You must let me make the decision.'

'You will get your reward in heaven.'

'I'm in no hurry to get there. You must still let me make the decision.'

'Then make it.'

'We will carry him. *And* his mother,' Caesar said.

There are four of us now. And the assorted animals. Not to mention God. *And* his mother. There is going to be only one voice, and that is mine, he thought. He went back to the cages. He scrutinized the occupants. The two apes were entwined like replete lovers. Nature hadn't constructed them for a long walk. Caesar looked at Lucrezia. She yawned, showing her sagging belly. She sounded like an old crone warming herself by the fire. She is getting fat. And lazy, Caesar thought.

He said to Maria, 'She is going to have to walk. Will she run away?'

'No. She is scared to be by herself,' Maria said.

Caesar opened the cage. He beckoned. Lucrezia looked at him reproachfully, her eyes widening like large green lamps. 'Out,' Caesar said. 'We have another tenant for your cage.' The tiger mewed. She walked out. The two nuns flinched.

Caesar led the mules into the garden. He put his shoulder to the statue. It was hollow plaster. It wasn't as heavy as he thought. He loosened up the straw in the cage. It smelled, rather. 'It is the best we can do. I hope God won't mind straw.'

'I am sure not. He was born in a manger,' Mother Beatrice said.

He roped up the statue. He put his jacket as a skid under the base. The two donkeys dragged it up into the cage. Caesar roped it firmly in place. The virgin was at peace. The child peered at him friendlily through the bars.

46

He arranged some softer seating for the two nuns on the roof. They climbed up. They looked precarious on the perch. He saw Sister Ursula cross herself secretly. Mother Beatrice said calmly, 'When you are ready, my son.'

Caesar flicked the reins. The cages rattled on their way.

The road was heaving steadily to the distant hills. The landscape grew bleak. The lusher trees went; tall forbidding pines took their place. On and on, through the later afternoon, the road wound. There were great chasms in the forest depths. Trees, taller than any building Caesar had ever seen, leaned like tired drunks. Some were uprooted. The topsoil had shifted, and underneath it the raw granite bulged. Down in the valley a river had changed its course. It dripped like a burst pipe into the forest; the old bed was dry and yellow. The road was scarred, but the litter didn't bar the mules. The cages rocked along. Mother Beatrice was getting used to her perch. Sister Ursula would never get used to it. They looked like the hardy women pioneers who went out west in covered wagons.

The light began to fade. Dusk fell. Caesar felt hungry. They had come quite a long way. He spoke to the mules and they stopped. He peered up the arid slopes. The birds sang in the unutterable loneliness. 'This will do for the night,' he said. The nuns got down stiffly. Maria stretched her young limbs and got down, too. Even the dancing donkeys grew still. Lucrezia squatted petulantly by the cages. She didn't like walking. She licked her paws.

Caesar loaded the shotgun. The loaf of bread he'd retrieved from the caravan wouldn't go far. The weapon made him feel invincible. He said confidently, 'There'll soon be supper,' and walked off along the dusky road. He listened to the cawing in the trees. He wasn't averse to stewed rook. Half a dozen would do. As he took aim he could almost smell the fragrance of the stewpot. There was a click. He

47

ejected the shell. There was no firing pin. The hammer was defective.

He went back. He dropped the shotgun in front of Maria. 'Your father never shot anything with this.'

'Nobody said he did. He kept it to scare off robbers.'

'That's useful.' His stomach felt as empty as a squeezed accordion. He squatted at the verge.

'We won't starve.' Mother Beatrice watched him keenly. 'It will be provided.'

He looked at her, thinking: the old are never hungry. I'm hungry most of the time.

'It just needs a little faith. Remember,' she reminded him softly. 'The widow's cruse was replenished.'

He didn't know what a cruse was. He didn't even know any widows.

Sister Ursula went into a flurry. She told Caesar about Elijah and the widow's cruse. She knew Kings I and II almost by heart. She ended up, quoting raptly, 'The cruse of oil shall not fail until the Lord sendeth rain upon the earth.' And her worn face lit up like a lamp.

Caesar thought the story curiously medieval. He didn't want to hurt her feelings by saying so. He got up and walked round to the back of the rear cage.

He leaned in on the straw. 'Listen, God,' he said confidentially. He kept his voice down. 'What is all this about faith?'

There was a moon coming up. It was velvety on the plaster. The shadow of the bars fell on the child's face.

'I'm a practical man,' Caesar said. 'Faith doesn't fill bellies. It fills churches. I'm not a church. And I have three foolish women on my hands.'

Maria had lighted a fire. The twigs crackled. The red glow flickered through the bars. It flowed across the virgin's face and she smiled. The child's eyes danced.

Caesar waited. 'You're not very talkative, are you?'

Mother Beatrice had good ears. She caught her breath with shock. She listened intently.

She heard him sigh, 'Don't you have anything to say? Frankly, I'm a little disappointed.'

The virgin looked at him with understanding. The child's eyes glinted like points of fire.

Caesar shrugged. 'A man has to depend on himself.' He crawled off the straw. 'Don't be offended. You're very young to be God. Maybe when you're older you'll be better at the business,' he said.

Maria had released the apes from their cage. They could forage for twigs and berries themselves. She couldn't depend on them to return; apes have a misguided love of freedom. Caesar listened to the gaoler's rattle as they skipped into the trees, each at the end of a long chain. Maria now nudged Lucrezia sharply. 'Get up,' she said. The tiger yawned. She was arthritic. She expected to be fed. 'Go and find yourself something to eat.'

Caesar said with surprise, 'By herself?'

'How do you think tigers lived in the jungle? When we were on the road my father always turned her out to get her own food.'

Caesar took her by the scruff of her neck. 'Perhaps she can get something for us, too,' he said.

They went into the thicket. He felt rather Babylonian. He'd seen pictures of square-bearded monarchs hunting with mountain lions. We will get armfuls of rabbits, he thought.

The boles of the trees ran with them. His eyes grew accustomed to the gloaming. Lucrezia left Caesar suddenly. She was very slow. But there were a great many rabbits. None of them anticipated tigers. When Caesar caught up with Lucrezia he found her slitting one of them neatly. He let her feed. 'Now one for us,' he said.

It took her ten minutes to find the next. He slipped it out

of her toothless mouth before she could eat it. 'Fair shares,' he said. It was a very small rabbit. It wouldn't make much of a meal.

The glade was suddenly empty of them. Lucrezia prowled about. She pounced here and there. She found nothing. Age had dulled her huntress's instinct. Perhaps the night damp had got into her bones. It was useless. Caesar led her back.

'It's all right.' He patted her. He felt sorry for her. 'There's no need to be ashamed. We all get past it,' he said.

He gave the rabbit to Maria. 'Here. Cook it. I'm not hungry.'

'You must be.'

'I had a good breakfast.' He'd had no breakfast. He hadn't eaten since the magistrate's bread and sausage last night. It seemed as far off in time as the Borgias. 'Don't argue,' he said.

He climbed up on the roof of the cage and lay down. The rabbit, hissing over the fire, made his saliva glands run. It was hardly bigger than a dormouse. He drew in his hollow stomach. He unwrapped Caesar Imperator's head. He ran his fingers possessively over the smooth marble. 'We have a different kind of faith,' he said to it in an intimate whisper. 'Faith in ourselves. Not in God. Who is ten years younger than myself.' The clear stone eyes stared sympathetically into his. 'We are men of action. From now on we act. Or starve. And we are *not* going to starve,' he said.

He got ready to sleep. The apes came back. They slipped into their cage and got ready to sleep, too. Caesar looked up at the vast glitter of the stars. He'd always thought God dwelt somewhere up there. It was odd to think of him sitting with his mother in the cage below. There was no breeze. The night was still. It was so still that the whine approaching over the hills made him prick his ears. It was faint at first. It grew louder. He knew the sound of the diesels and he sat up. He saw Maria point suddenly up the slope, heard her whisper to the two nuns. There was a road somewhere in the heights. The glare of the headlamps lighted the sky as if aircraft were wheeling in the darkness.

The convoy was here.

The din ceased. The dazzle remained. Then there was the pink glow of fires. They were making camp for the night.

Caesar got down. He was frantic with hunger. The two nuns nibbled bread. The rabbit cooking over the fire wouldn't have fed a child. 'I'm beginning to believe in miracles.' Caesar stared up the dark slope. It was terribly steep. He would have climbed Vesuvius for food. 'They will give us something to eat,' he said.

He started the ascent. He felt something large and hairy at his side. 'Not you,' he whispered. It was Lucrezia. 'Go back.' She seemed to have grown attached to him. She climbed on at his side. It was a long way up. His feet dislodged stones. They rattled like avalanches below.

They stopped for breath at the top. Lucrezia panted. Ten years of fairground performing hadn't improved her condition. It had become an effort to jump through a hoop.

The convoy was parked a hundred metres along the road. The wind whistled up here. Cooking fires crackled. Caesar heard the chatter of voices in the darkness. He walked towards the camp.

Lucrezia padded ahead. The wind carried the scent of veal and spaghetti: it was delicious. She was hungry, too. She came out of the dark like an apparition. The men, sprawled about the fires, froze. The first thing they saw was the baleful glow of her green eyes. There was a quick instinctive Italian scamper for guns. Lucrezia passed the Pirelli family at supper. Luigi's wife screamed. It ululated horridly through the camp.

It made Lucrezia nervous. She swerved out of the glare of the headlamps. The scream raised the hairs on

Major-General Brazzolo's neck. He came from behind a truck. They met head on. He shrank from the heavy striped body. He stared into Lucrezia's neon-bright eyes. He was a highly emotional man. He had no time for thought: only for liquid fear. He reached for his pistol like a sleepwalker and shot her dead.

VI

HE was sorry the moment he'd done it. He looked at the grey old muzzle. The thing was a loose furry envelope containing a heap of bones. He averted his eyes from the trickle of blood.

He thought wildly: they have no right to look at me like that. I carry the responsibility of the whole camp.

The men gathered silently about. They put their rifles away guiltily. It wasn't even worth a bullet. It looked like a rather mangy rug.

Then the boy came up. He stood staring at it with a curious stillness.

Major-General Brazzolo mopped his neck. He sweated with shame. I am getting too fat: I must lose a little weight, he thought.

He didn't know what to say. He had to say something. 'It was a ferocious beast,' he stammered.

Sergeant Naso pulled the muzzle away from the gums. 'She has no teeth. The thing is older than Methuselah's sister. As ferocious as a kitten,' he said.

'Mind your own business.'

'Yes, major-general.'

Lieutenant Arnolfo said nothing. He was watching the boy.

Caesar looked at the pistol. He could smell the cordite at six paces.

The major-general had the uneasy feeling that if the boy got hold of it he would shoot him. He put it away.

'The animal had no right to be here,' he said defiantly. 'It could have torn somebody to pieces.'

'My wife,' Luigi said. He had just come up. He was trembling. He got ready to steal the stage. 'The beast passed us. At this distance.' He measured off a hair's breadth with his twittering fingers. He poked up a thumb. It was symbolic of death. 'Its teeth were bared. I saw them.' And his fingers crooked vampire-fashion to suggest naked fangs. The soldiers watched with fascination. There were some good Italian hand-talkers amongst them. But nobody like this. Sergeant Naso looked at him with contempt. He'd just said that the tiger had no teeth.

'You are a fool,' he said.

'I saw them.'

'Be quiet, actor. You will poke somebody's eyes out with those hands.'

Lieutenant Arnolfo said gently to Caesar, 'What was it you wanted?'

The boy spoke for the first time. 'Food,' he said.

'Of course. Where is the girl?'

'Down the slope.'

'I am sorry about your animal.' The lieutenant wished he could soften the blow. He didn't like the cold look in the boy's eyes.

Caesar went over to Lucrezia. He bent. He felt the fur. She was still warm. He tugged experimentally at one of the whiskers as if the momentary pain might bring her to life. The heavy head lolled. And the sea-green old eyes looked glazedly into his. Caesar had never been really close to death. It revolted him. He thought: this is all waste. She wasn't a good rabbit-chaser. She wasn't even good at jumping through hoops. But she gave a little pleasure. She was my friend. What am I to say to Maria? I let her come with me. I made myself responsible for her. And I let her come to her death.

It was a very involved mental argument. What his furious

young brain really thought was: this fat major-general butchered her. I would like to butcher him.

He got up. 'Why did you do it?'

The major-general couldn't think why he should have to defend himself. 'This is a military camp. We cannot have wild animals roaming . . .'

'Answer one question at a time. Why did you do it?'

'Don't address me like that.'

'I am not afraid of your brass.'

The soldiers watched. They weren't afraid of his brass, either. The major-general wished to God they would go away. 'Get rid of it,' he said angrily to Sergeant Naso.

The blood had spread in a glutinous pool under the head. Major-General Brazzolo wouldn't have confessed to his parish priest that the sight of blood made him feel faint.

'How, major-general?'

The major-general shouted, 'Don't ask stupid questions. Throw it over the cliff.'

Lieutenant Arnolfo winced. He thought it terribly tactless. He could have buried the thing later.

Sergeant Naso beckoned. Four of the men took it gingerly by the paws and dragged it to the verge. It slurred unpleasantly. It left a red trail like a squashed bug. They shoved and it went toppling into the darkness. They heard it plop after a long while like a wet bag.

Lieutenant Arnolfo looked at the boy's bitter, offended face, thinking: he's very young. But he will make a bad enemy. His name isn't Caesar for nothing. I wouldn't like to get on the wrong side of him.

He has the makings of a good soldier, Sergeant Naso thought. He is a good hater. Good soldiers had to be good haters. He has iron guts. That was another thing good soldiers had to have. Iron guts.

Luigi felt that he was losing the limelight. 'Major-general, it was an act of lightning courage.' Little fingers hooked for lightning, one big scoop of the hands for courage . . .

'Shut up,' the major-general said. He didn't like the expression on the boy's face, either.

'You should be in a slaughterhouse,' Caesar said.

'Will you be quiet?'

'Butcher.'

The major-general wiped his neck. I am one vast reservoir of sweat, he thought.

'Boy. Watch your tongue.'

'And what will you do if I don't? Tell your sergeant to throw me over the cliff?'

'Dismiss,' the major-general said to his men. They moved off a few paces. They didn't want to miss a word.

'All right,' Caesar said. 'So now be careful.'

He found himself trembling. All his twelve years, as far back as he could remember, and he could almost remember the vague blur that had been his mother's face, he'd suffered slights and hunger. Cuffs about the head. The priest saying, 'Pagan.' It had turned him into a militant. He suddenly needed an enemy. Somebody to sharpen his claws on. The major-general had walked tailor-made into the part. Caesar looked at the sad, hot, plump, mottled face and thought: I will burst him like a balloon.

'Watch out for me. Wherever you are, whenever I see you, I will make your life a misery for you,' he said.

'Enough,' Lieutenant Arnolfo said. He began to feel sorry for the major-general. He took hold of the boy's shoulder. 'That will do.'

'I have declared war on the whole Italian army.'

Sergeant Naso chuckled. He *is* a good hater. He doesn't mind taking on long odds.

'Big talker,' he said roughly. 'Run along.'

He was tempted to help him a little with his boot.

'Remember.' Caesar walked off. He looked back. He was

very small. The last thing they saw of him in the wavering firelight was his torn pants: it was ludicrous. They saw him wipe his fingers. They didn't know that he had Lucrezia's blood on them. 'The whole Italian army,' they heard him call back. 'I have declared war on you.' And then he was gone.

The soldiers drifted off. It had been rather odd. I am sorry about the whole thing, the lieutenant thought. Big mouth, the sergeant thought amusedly. Give him to me for ten years. I could make something good of him.

Caesar walked on down the road. The wind was keen. He shivered a little. He passed the parked trucks. The idea was only a ghost in his mind as he paused to look into them, one by one. Some had complicated equipment. Some were stacked with canned rations. Soldiers fed well. Veal. Vermicelli. Beans. Beans were the military basic belly-filler. And Caesar's belly burped emptily. The idea became suddenly cold and clear and vengeful in his mind.

He glanced back at the blobs that were the men sprawled, chattering, about the fires. He got into a truck. He had driven Luigi's ancient Ford. It was a museum specimen. But they all worked on a common principle. There was a gear shift that was more or less complicated: a clutch and a brake pedal. He could just reach them with his feet. He had to study the dashboard to find the starter. He started the motor. It caught.

None of the men responded to the roar. There was always some mechanic fiddling with a motor, though not usually at this time of night. Only Sergeant Naso thought curiously: what is this? He saw the truck move out of formation. It had no lights. It ground fast down the road. And now, even more curiously, he thought: why? The truck vanished into the night. He heard the squeal of brakes. He couldn't see it now.

Caesar was taking a great risk. He guessed the position of

the cages somewhere below. He dropped the tailboard and reversed the truck hard towards the verge. Then stood on the brake pedal. It jarred. The shock loosened every can in the back. He did it again. Forward, then back, braking violently as it bumped on the verge. It could have taken him to his death over the edge. The wheels skidded. The cans leapt out of the back with the impetus and an avalanche of them went clattering down the slope.

Caesar thought: I hope they are arriving like manna from heaven. Now we will eat.

He got out of the truck and went slithering down the grass after the cans.

He had chosen the point of discharge well. The first can came down the slope like a missile and rebounded from the bars of the cages. Numbers One and Two whined. They withdrew from a careless embrace. (They were insatiable.) The donkeys jumped. Most of the cans found an eternal resting place on the bleak hillside. About fifteen of them bombed the cages and littered the road. Maria picked one up. Sister Ursula cried out, 'Manna from heaven.' It was in the form of vermicelli. She believed it, too.

They were gathering them together as Caesar arrived. He was scratched from the descent down the coarse vegetation. He looked furious. Maria began, 'What have you . . .?'

'Eat,' he said. 'And hurry. I am hungry.'

'Where is Lucrezia?'

'Dead.' He made the announcement coolly. Maria's mouth opened. Almost soundlessly she wept. She saw him looking at his hands. He rubbed hard and angrily at the red stains. 'Ask no questions. Eat,' he said.

He guessed that they would have visitors by and by. There was time for veal and vermicelli. He hacked open two cans. Mother Beatrice stoked up the fire. She watched him narrowly. This is a whirlwind of a boy: a fury. God will have questions to put to him, she thought.

They ate. Caesar watched the firelight dancing up the stark hillside. He wondered where Lucrezia lay. He hoped she would find hoops to jump through in heaven. She had to come all the way from Africa to feed the buzzards of the Abruzzi. (She was Indian.) I will remember that fat major-general, he thought.

He finished the scrapings of a can. He sighed. His belly was filled. 'I am tired,' he said simply. The wind whistled along the defile. 'Now I am going to sleep.'

He went back to the rear cage. 'No need to move,' he said to the virgin. 'There is room for three of us.' The child watched him. 'If God has no objection.' He loosened up the straw and crept in. Mother Beatrice wrapped her gown about her. Sister Ursula dozed.

Maria lay down under the apes' cage. They were never still for an instant. There was a friendly scuffling like amorous mice over her head. Castor and Pollux gazed into the windy distance, dreaming of dancing music. The mules did nothing. Given the opportunity, mules will always do nothing.

There was the hum of a motor. Caesar had guessed that they would find a way down from the heights. Head-lights poked like feelers along the road. They rested on the cages. They had the blinding look of nemesis. The staff-car stopped.

Major-General Brazzolo was in a highly confused state. He still smarted from the incident with the tiger. Guilt is bad for fat, overwrought men. The boy's cold abrasive voice had humiliated him. Humiliation on top of guilt is like petrol poured on fire. He had seen the truck with its rear wheels perched on the verge. It was hair-raising. Cans littered the slope. Military rations had gone down there. The major-general had the precise mind of a regimental

59

storekeeper. 'Get them back,' he said to Lieutenant Arnolfo in a thick voice.

'Yes, major-general.'

'It is theft. They are army property.'

'A few cans . . .?'

'It is a matter of principle. I am responsible for the detachment's inventory. I cannot trust you. Sergeant Naso,' he shouted. 'I will see to it myself.'

He got out of the staff-car. He walked across to the cages. He didn't see the nuns resting in the ditch. He picked up an empty can by the fire. It infuriated him. He stirred Maria. 'Girl,' he said accusingly. 'Where did this come from?'

'It fell down the hill.'

'Fell?' He contained himself. 'Thrown,' he said.

'We were sitting here when . . .'

'Where is the boy?'

'Sleeping.'

'He will sleep behind bars.' Which, oddly enough, was exactly where Caesar was sleeping. Suddenly two white head-dresses rose from the ditch. The major-general stared at the two nuns. He was a devout man. He began uneasily, 'Sister . . .'

'Mother Beatrice. What can be wrong?'

'This food was stolen.'

'Ah. I am sorry to hear that.'

'The boy . . .'

'We ate a little. That must make us accomplices.'

'No, no. You are welcome.'

'But not the child?' Mother Beatrice glanced at Maria.

'Her, too.'

'And the boy? We were hungry.'

'He had no right to . . .' and the major-general felt himself at a moral disadvantage. He looked angrily at Sergeant Naso. He walked to the back of the other cage. The boy lay in the straw. He had strange company. The major-general stared at the virgin and the child. He crossed himself instinctively. He was sure the boy wasn't sleeping. The nuns were gathering together the rest of the cans. He called back, 'Please. There is no need to . . .'

'We must return them.'

'No. Keep them.' The major-general believed that it was a sin to deprive the hungry religious of food. 'We have plenty.'

'We would prefer it. God will provide.'

'He has,' Major-General Brazzolo said. Through the commissariat of the Italian army. By the medium of that demon of a boy. He could hardly keep the frustration out of his voice. 'It is all right. It is our pleasure.' He saw Sergeant Naso twinkling. He went back to the car.

The sergeant went to look at the boy in the cage. He *knew* he wasn't sleeping. He nudged him. 'You,' he said. 'Big mouth. Wake up.'

Caesar opened his eyes.

'That was a crazy thing to do with the truck. Another metre and you would have gone over the edge.'

'But I didn't.'

'Next time, maybe. There is always hope. You are making the major-general very angry.'

'Good. I have declared war on him. On you, too. The whole Italian army.'

'All right, enemy,' the sergeant said. The boy was holding something closely. It glimmered. 'What have you got there?'

'My *imperator*.' Caesar showed the marble head.

'Oh, him.' The sergeant stared at it curiously. 'The big Julius. His kind doesn't come twice.'

'What makes you so sure?'

'You fancy yourself, don't you?' The sergeant chuckled. 'Big mouth.' He went back to the car.

Caesar watched him drive the major-general off. He said softly to the *imperator*, 'It was a victory. There will be others. Let him watch out.' He thought the virgin was looking at him rather regretfully. Her son's face seemed sad. Women don't understand these things. And he is too young, he thought. He nestled deep in the straw and went to sleep.

VII

HE woke early. It was still quite dark. He was chilled to the marrow. A grey mist was rolling down the defile. He shook off the straw and said *'Buon giorno'* politely to God. A dew like frigid little pearls had formed on the child's face. He feels it, too, Caesar thought. The mother leaned over him, infusing warmth. 'It isn't a very nice morning. Not to worry. There will be a sun later,' he reassured them. 'It will take the cold out of your bones.'

He was glad they weren't making the journey in winter. The Abruzzi could be neck-deep in snow.

He went first to see to the mules. They would be lost without them. They watched him with hostility. He rubbed their knees to unstiffen them. They made internal noises. Nobody ever gets love from a mule, he thought.

Castor and Pollux grazed under the stars. They danced now and again, as if hearing heavenly music. It was purely a reflex action. Caesar thought them simple-minded. He looked in at the apes. Number One slept with Number Two in his arms.

These preliminary duties done, he went into the bushes for his private business.

Then he stirred Maria with his foot. 'Up,' he said softly.

She was instantly awake. 'So early?' She shivered. She looked at the stars.

'We have a long way to go.'

'Couldn't we sleep a little longer?'

'Sleep in Rome.'

She sighed. 'You are ruthless.' She soaked her handkerchief in dew and wiped her face.

63

He blew up the embers of last night's fire. He boiled a little water in a can that had contained beans. It tasted interestingly of soup. He saw the two nuns rise stiffly from the ditch. Both were haggard. Mother Beatrice said in a cracked voice, 'If you will give us a few moments.' He thought it was for a rather personal business. In a sense it was. They withdrew into a kind of spiritual privacy. He listened to their muttered devotions. The rosaries clicked. He found it strange. He thought: God is over there in the cage. Why can't they talk to him face to face?

They came to the fire. They looked old and cold. He opened another can of veal. 'It is all we can spare,' he said. 'There is not much food.'

'We are used to fasting.'

'Two meals a day must be enough.'

'You know best, my son.'

'Yes,' he said. He nodded calmly. He thought so, too. The fire crackled. The stars paled. A razor-edge of blue crept into the sky. Suddenly there was a gritty roar up in the heights. They would soon be leaving up there, too. They were warming up the tank-transports. He stopped eating to listen with his head reared like a cobra.

'Why are you so angry?' Maria asked.

'Who said I am angry?'

'You should see your face.'

'These people are our enemies.'

'The soldiers? What did they . . . ?'

'The fat one. Brazzolo. The major-general. Him with the brass.'

Maria said coolly, 'You must like enemies. You are pitiless. I feel sorry for that poor fat man.'

He stared at her. 'You are mad.'

'We have enough trouble. We have to survive.' And she reminded him, 'We have to take God back to Rome.'

'I will get God to Rome.'

'Is there no more veal? I am hungry.'

'Discipline yourself. You are going to have a hollow belly for five days.' He got up. He kicked away the cans. He said, 'You are very soft.' She had annoyed him. 'You are a woman. You do not have a man's pride.' And he looked at her coldly and went to hitch up the mules.

Mother Beatrice said softly to Maria, 'He is like a coiled spring.' Her eyes shone.

Maria shrugged. 'Boys.' She was more cynical.

'He is no ordinary boy.'

'He is a pint-pot. He isn't properly grown up. He thinks he can shove the world along.'

'He may. One day.'

'Let it come. I am worried about today. Not tomorrow. We are stuck here. With the earth all broken and shaking.' Maria was a practical young woman. 'Let him shove us along,' she said.

Caesar finished hitching up the mules. One of them snapped at him. It didn't soften his mood. He went to the rear cage and rummaged under the straw for the *imperator*. 'Big Julius,' he said appreciatively, recollecting the sergeant. He rather liked the name. He felt that he could confide in it. They were more of a kind. 'We have three women with us,' he said. 'They are going to be very trying.'

He looked up. God's mother, bent over him, seemed to be bent over him, too. She was somehow too tranquil to be classified as a 'trying woman'. 'No reflection on you, madam,' he said.

And he went on confiding in the marble, 'They are all right for cooking. For bearing children. But if you let them, they will blunt a man's resolution.'

The marble flashed. The sun was coming up. 'You are so right,' the fiercely arrogant eyes seemed to say. 'I had a little trouble with women, too.'

For two thousand years history had been dramatizing

Big Julius' trouble with the plump sensualist of Egypt. That Cleopatra!

'I hacked out an empire.' The stone eyes brooded. 'It stretched from Persia to Gaul. Because I was a man of action. With me it was action first, then thought. Let God do the thinking. I *acted*! That was why my shadow lay like a colossus across the world.'

The sun, creeping higher, caught the child's face. It flashed for a moment, too.

'Discipline. Order. And authority,' the intractable stone eyes told Caesar.

'I understand. These things are the heart and guts of a man,' Caesar said.

'Be strong. And pitiless. The rest will follow.'

'I will remember,' Caesar said.

The virgin flowed with the pink of the rising sun. It was probably a trick of the light. She looked strangely agitated, too.

Caesar heard a soft scrape. There was someone behind him. Mother Beatrice was leaning into the cage.

'Who is it you are talking to?' she asked.

Caesar hesitated. It was too late to hide it. He let her see the marble. 'Big Julius,' he said.

'Oh. That one.' She stared at it curiously. 'He *was* big, wasn't he?'

'I think so.'

'He was also cruel. He terrorized the peoples of the earth.'

Caesar found himself going on the defensive. 'A man is what he has to be.'

'A man has to be what he chooses.' Mother Beatrice looked up at the virgin and automatically crossed herself. Then she looked at the child and said, 'They lived in the same times. He and Caesar. One was love. One was terror. Which of them, do you think, was really big?'

Caesar measured the child with his eye for size. 'He doesn't look very big to me.'

'He is bigger than the human heart understands.'

Caesar thrust Big Julius under the straw. She is an old woman with all the fury of living burned out of her, he thought. We do not talk the same language. He withdrew into the shell of his dignity. 'It is time to go.'

'We are ready.'

He mounted the leading cage. He took the mules' reins. Maria was about to get up beside him when Mother Beatrice waved her back. 'If I might ride with him. It would be a change.'

Caesar sighed to himself: she isn't going to let go. He didn't want to offend her. 'It is better behind. The mules smell.'

She twinkled. 'They are God's creatures.'

It wasn't an argument. He was also one of God's creatures. And he didn't smell. He got down reluctantly and helped her up. He heard her joints creak. She is *ancient*, he thought.

There was a vast belch of sound from up in the heights. The convoy was on the move. Caesar sat listening to the thunder of the diesels. The ground trembled with them even down in the defile. 'We have only mules,' he said. He whipped them along. His eyes shone belligerently. 'But we will be ahead of them in the end.'

'We will all reach our journey's end,' Mother Beatrice said. 'God willing.'

'We have him in our cage. He is on our side,' Caesar said.

The mules strained. The effort produced one of those intestinal convulsions. Mother Beatrice winced. They *did* smell. The cages rattled off. Castor and Pollux pranced alongside.

The din of the convoy faded into the upper distance. We will meet again, Caesar thought. All roads lead to Rome. I haven't finished with them yet.

67

Mother Beatrice said gently, 'You have very passionate feelings.' She watched him sidelong.

'That is so. Hup, hup,' he said to the mules.

'How old are you?'

'Twelve.'

'It is a wonderful age to be.'

'I think so, too.' Caesar took a quick look at her. This is where we start getting the morning sermon. 'Move, you horrible smelly creatures,' he said to the mules.

'One must govern one's passion. It can be both a great servant and a cruel master,' she said.

'I intend to be the master. Don't worry,' Caesar said.

'Then love them.'

'Who?'

'Our friends up there. Who have just departed. They fed us.'

'*I* fed you,' Caesar corrected her coolly. 'I helped myself to the cans.'

'There is a commandment . . .'

'So I have heard. There are ten of them. The priest in the village accused me of breaking twenty.'

'Did you not perhaps provoke him?'

'I don't know. I never went to church.'

'Nothing else?'

'I am a bastard. Is there a commandment about that?'

'No.' Mother Beatrice swallowed. She was trying to get hold of his soul. And it squirmed evasively in her hand. 'There is an eleventh commandment. Love one another.'

'Ten are enough for me,' he said. Too many if anything. There was one prior commandment. Be strong: and fulfil yourself.

The mules gasped. The road went spiralling up. The cages jolted as if they would come apart. The sun glared. But the air grew chill. The scene was as forbidding as Dante's inferno. It was all slabbed stone, as steep as the sides of skyscrapers; they rattled through awesome gorges that echoed the crunch of the wheels. Not even a charcoal-burner came up here. There were a few trees. The shocks had loosened them. They drooped like surrendered flags.

Caesar stole a look at Mother Beatrice. 'Who am I supposed to love? Everybody?' he asked.

She knew where it was leading. She wasn't going to fall into the trap.

'All men are brothers.'

'I don't know that many men,' he said. 'I just know the priest. I wouldn't want him as a brother. I know Luigi Pirelli. I would want him even less.' His voice rose scornfully. 'That Brazzolo. Is he supposed to be my brother, too?'

'Of course.'

'Why? He is stupid.'

'He means well. He carries the responsibility for many lives. He is under great strain.'

'How does a man like that come to be a major-general? He is too fat.'

Mother Beatrice struggled with her emotions. Perhaps the air was too thin for her. She began to feel a little faint.

She found her tongue. 'In the name of him you carry behind, learn to show men kindness.'

'What for? It would be silly. Men are not kind. They come into the world greedy. They reach for what they can grab. He is my enemy,' Caesar said.

'No, no.' She gave him an appalled look.

'I am going to test myself against him,' he said. 'A man is like a knife. He has to sharpen himself all the time. I am going to sharpen myself on that fat Brazzolo. I am going to make his life a misery. I am going to beat him into the earth with every opportunity I have.'

The road was choked like a demolition site with the debris of the earthquake. The mules rode it like goats.

'For the love of God,' Mother Beatrice burst out.

'Does he love everybody, too?' Caesar asked.

'Everybody.'

'There are an awful lot of people. He can't be very selective. He is spreading his love a little thin.'

He caught sight of Mother Beatrice's face. He felt sorry for her.

She was thinking with horror: Big Julius probably had a caustic tongue like that. But this boy has freshness and ardour, there is a sunshine in him that Big Julius never had.

'Don't be upset,' Caesar said kindly. 'You have lived with women too long. You do not understand the world.'

Sister Ursula, sitting behind, was so attuned to Mother Beatrice that she could feel the turmoil in her heart. It was a kind of spiritual telepathy. She stiffened. She gripped Maria's hand. 'What is going on there?' she cried.

'You are hurting me.'

'What is he saying to her?'

'How do I know? He is very self-willed.'

'Heaven will teach him humility.'

Maria gave her an odd look. Heaven would have its work cut out. 'Nobody will ever teach him humility,' she said.

Caesar was right. Mother Beatrice had lived with women too long. She often regretted the sterility of her existence. She stared at him intensely. She felt the overwhelming challenge. I will redeem this boy, she thought.

He wasn't worried about his spiritual future. He was listening to the asthmatic panting of the mules. The air really was getting very thin. Even the donkeys were too winded to dance. They went rattling through gullies as awesome as the gateway to hell. 'Hup,' he said to the mules, and it bounced back at him off the crags in a great yammering HUP HUP HUP. He chuckled. He tried it again. Mother Beatrice wished he wouldn't. The vista down there was terrible. She was afraid of heights.

Caesar knew what he was looking for. He expected to see it soon. They came on it suddenly. There was a telegraph pole on the skyline. It leaned drunkenly. It trailed broken wire.

The mules dragged the cages up on to the highway. Caesar let them rest. He got down and stared at the road.

It puzzled him. The convoy must have passed this way. He should have seen the tracks of the great tank-transports. And there wasn't a sign. He wondered with mild optimism if they were having trouble.

They were. The convoy, in fact, was still ten kilometres back along the bleak road. To the end of his days Major-General Brazzolo would remember this journey as a personal ordeal: and his purgatory really began today.

There is this legend of Sisyphus. He was made to push uphill a huge rock, which fell back as soon as it reached the top. Like Sisyphus, the men felt that they were patching up something that fell to pieces as they went along. It is the kind of frustrative punishment that drives mythological heroes mad. Italians aren't mythological. They have too much humour to be heroes. They cursed like demons. Italian is a good language for cursing. The shocks that had broken the mountain had splintered the road like glass. Sergeant Naso was a wise old sweat. He knew that they were near the flashpoint of explosion. He even dirtied his fingers a little, helping out. Lieutenant Arnolfo was limp with exhaustion. Under his uniform Major-General Brazzolo was a sodden mash of sweat.

Round about mid-morning the convoy rested. They had a little soup. The cooks were too tired to prepare a meal. Major-General Brazzolo sat with Lieutenant Arnolfo, watching the half-naked men muttering. There was a staring sullenness about them. 'What is the matter with them?' the major-general asked Sergeant Naso when he came over with their bowls of soup.

'Let them blow off steam, major-general. Soldiers always grumble.'

'I will not have my men grumbling.'

The sergeant shrugged. Nobody could stop soldiers grumbling. Particularly Italian soldiers.

'They are scared,' he said.

The major-general flushed. 'Soldiers aren't supposed to be scared.'

This is a civilian myth. Soldiers are ordinary people. They usually have more reason to be scared than most.

'They say we will never reach Naples alive,' the sergeant said.

'They are mad.'

'Yes, major-general.'

'Of course we will reach Naples. Do you doubt it?'

'No, major-general.' The sergeant was seriously beginning to doubt it. He was a little scared, too.

Lieutenant Arnolfo met his eyes. There was something else. He could see it.

'What has got into them?'

'They say we are running out of luck,' the sergeant said.

'Luck?' the major-general burst out. 'What has luck got to do with it?' He was a technical officer. Technicians do not believe in luck. 'Are you crazy, too?'

'They think somebody is wishing us bad.'

'There is nothing bad but an earthquake. People survive.'

Sergeant Naso, who had seen the results of the earthquake on the villagers of Lorenzo of the Angels, remembered that scarcely any of them had survived.

At that moment there was a sudden enraged shouting amongst the men. The sergeant didn't like the sound of it. He ran back.

What had happened was this. A certain Private Moro had gone to the end of the convoy to relieve himself. He was in full view of the truck containing the Pirelli family.

He was too exhausted to care. Glancing up, he saw Luigi Pirelli's wife glaring at him. She had a facial affliction. She had a tic in her cheek. Private Moro saw her twitching eye fixed on him. It was malevolent. She happened to be muttering. She had been praying. She was still counting her beads. He was in the nervous state to believe anything. He moved off two paces and shouted, 'She has the evil eye.'

Luigi Pirelli's wife said angrily, 'Fiend. In front of my daughter. You should be ashamed.'

'Look at her. She is cursing us,' Private Moro said.

The men gathered. They stared at her. She became agitated. The tic under her eye jumped convulsively. They were a Sicilian detachment. They were collectively as super-stitious as pagans. They came from villages dominated by medieval priests and the Mafia: most of them carried some kind of pewter saint to bring them luck. A few carried amulets blessed by local white witches. They believed in black witches, too. This woman was one. The tic is generally recognized as a malignant sign.

Luigi Pirelli said, 'To perform in front of my daughter. She is an innocent.' He acted out Private Moro's deed. 'It is an outrage against decency.'

'She is overlooking us,' one of the men said.

Overlooking meant: giving us the bad eye. It is a kind of optical curse.

'Tell them it is nonsense,' Major-General Brazzolo said to Sergeant Naso. He had just arrived. He was in despair. And this is twentieth-century Italy, he thought. 'She has a nervous affliction.'

'They have a nervous affliction, too. They are scared,' Sergeant Naso said.

'It is barbaric.'

Sergeant Naso studied the gleaming, twittering eye. It *looked* evil. He came from Syracuse, which is civilized. It is possible, he thought.

73

'Get them moving,' the major-general said.

'Back to the vehicles. At the double.' Sergeant Naso began to harry the men. They drew off. The major-general couldn't hear what they were saying. The Pirelli family finally got down from their truck.

Sergeant Naso came back. 'Nobody will drive them,' he said.

'Why not?'

'She would overlook them.'

The major-general looked helplessly at Lieutenant Arnolfo. 'Nobody would believe it. All right,' he said to Sergeant Naso. 'Put them in the staff-car. I will drive them myself.'

The incident had delayed them thirty minutes. At about this time Caesar arrived on the highway.

He helped Mother Beatrice and Sister Ursula down. Both were stiff to the point of martyrdom. The trembling mules sought a shady spot under a cliff. Castor and Pollux found the strength to skip. Numbers One and Two took advantage of the rest to indulge in matrimony. They were hampered on the journey by the jolting of the cage.

Caesar stared along the highway. A lower road forked off it. It went down to Utrelli. The top of the Abruzzi is riddled with roads like blue veins in cheese. He got on Castor's back and trotted for about twenty minutes along the highway. When he returned he was laughing. Mother Beatrice wondered why.

The convoy had come crawling round the bend. It drew up palpitatingly behind the cages. Caesar had left them in the middle of the road. He hitched up the mules. Mother Beatrice looked at him curiously. 'What has amused you, my son?'

'Nothing.'

'Then why are you laughing?'

'Don't ask him. He is a devil,' Maria said.

The major-general watched the cages move off along the highway. He was tempted, out of sheer contrariness, to take the lower road. But he had seen Caesar return on the donkey's back. He had obviously reconnoitred the highway. The major-general was tired. He couldn't think clearly. He hadn't had two good nights' sleep in a week. He looked round at the thudding convoy. There were moments when he felt the whole iron cortège like a hump on his back. Sergeant Naso watched him expressionlessly from his cab. Lieutenant Arnolfo wouldn't meet his eyes.

Nobody would help. The major-general sighed. He gave the signal to follow Caesar and the convoy ground on.

There was no room to overtake the cages. The road wound through the precipitous gully. The steep sides reverberated with the deafening roar. It held the fumes of the diesels like a tube. They suffered for twenty minutes. The major-general, glancing round, saw a twitching basilisk eye fixed on him. Luigi Pirelli's wife and daughter sat in the back. He felt a curious tremor. He closed the windows of the car. He couldn't breathe.

He had the sensation that the cliffs were closing in. The earthquake had shoved at them: they towered precipitously. The tube of the road was growing constricted. And suddenly there was scarcely room to scrape by. He heard an iron screech. The leading tank-transport was locked. Both sides were grazing stone. The driver had been foolish to try to shove through. He was caught like a cork in a bottle.

There was room for the cages and they rolled on. The major-general watched them blindly. He knew that he had been deliberately trapped. He got out. Half the detachment had descended. The smoke made the air stifling. They were trying to loosen the tank-transport from the grip of the stone. The gun shook with the vibration. Rocks fell from the cliffs and clattered on metal.

'Go back,' the major-general said. He was trembling with bitterness. The cages had disappeared.

It took them most of the afternoon to release the tank-transport. It was a frightful operation. They tore it loose: the monster, with its shaking gun, had to reverse. The whole convoy, in fact, began the return journey in reverse. It might have been comical, had it not been tragically arduous. They emerged from the road backwards, like a foetus from a womb.

Bastard, Sergeant Naso thought with grim affection. He was thinking of Caesar. Lieutenant Arnolfo remembered saying to himself: he will make a bad enemy. I wouldn't like to get on the wrong side of him, he told himself again.

Mother Beatrice had eyes. She had looked back. She had ears, too. She didn't hear the frantic cursing. The cages had taken her out of earshot. But she heard the rasping iron-on-stone commotion. She searched Caesar's face. She was ashamed of her suspicions. She said to him painfully, 'You knew it would happen?'

He didn't reply.

'You passed here on the donkey.'

'Perhaps,' he said.

'Was it not cruel?'

He looked at her squarely. 'Yes.'

'You could have warned them.'

'What for? It would have been silly. It is the first rule of war. You beat your enemy,' he said.

'They are not your enemies,' she stammered. She was losing control of herself. 'They are your . . .'

'. . . brothers. So you told me. I hardly knew my mother. If she had given me that Brazzolo for a brother I would have disowned her,' he said.

'Do you hate him?'

He considered it fairly. 'No.'

'What did he do?'

76

'He made me feel small. I am going to trample him down. To make myself big again,' he said.

It was hard to believe that she was listening to a stripling. Look at him. Twelve years of living: and talking like Big Julius.

'Stop it,' she gasped. Caesar looked at her. She had grown quite pale. 'Don't talk like that . . .'

'Why not? He hurt my pride.'

'Pride.' She was shouting. She hadn't shouted since she was a novice. That was fifty years back. The Mother-Superior of the day had given her ten days' bread-and-water in the kitchen. 'It is the devil's personal sin . . .'

'What is wrong with it? Isn't God proud?'

'Yes.' Mother Beatrice's mouth opened. 'But differently.' She was trembling. I must contain myself, she thought. She stared at him fascinatedly. She wondered who the unknown father was. The sun flashed like a neon about the extra-ordinarily fair hair. Hair like that was as rare in central Italy as the Hong-Kong dollar. She couldn't take her eyes off the resolute young face. Her heart swelled. This is a brand to be plucked from the burning. Mother Beatrice was an alert, forward-looking woman. But she sometimes used musty medieval expressions. Heaven has sent me to bring him to grace, she thought.

'Forgive me,' she said to him sweetly. 'I was over-wrought.'

'It's all right.' He cocked an eye at her. He couldn't understand this blowing hot-and-cold. 'You are a woman. Women are easily upset.'

'I will try not to be.'

'Tell God not to worry. I will get him to Rome.'

Her mouth twitched. 'I am sure of it.'

'It's a promise.' He clucked at the mules. They were beginning to hate each other. They weren't pulling in unison. 'I will see to him,' he said.

The mountain air made them ravenous. He opened two cans for supper. There were very few left. Mother Beatrice saw him counting them. She thought piously: heaven will give us food. He thought: I will have to beg, borrow or steal some. There was this difference in their approach. He turned the mules loose to forage. The rocks were bare. They looked cheated. He went back to the rear cage. He felt under the straw for Big Julius. The touch of it reassured him. He looked up at the virgin and chuckled wryly. 'It's a good thing you and God are not hungry. I couldn't feed another two appetites,' he said.

The thought occurred to him. He stared at the child and said, 'By the way, God. *Are* you proud?'

The soft young face flowed with shadow. He had the notion that it was saying something like: proud of the eternal hope of humanity. And it isn't really pride, is it? It's more a kind of joyful humility.

The shadow shifted and the virgin looked with intense feeling at Caesar.

'It's a hard world, God. Nobody survives without pride,' he said. He was a little disappointed in them. 'The humble go to the wall. I stand on my own two feet. I do not intend to be pushed to the wall.'

The virgin seemed to be desperate to say something. The child continued to watch him. Caesar felt the vibration of great emotion in the air.

'I am what I am. I will do what I am meant to do.' He rubbed Big Julius under the straw. 'I am small. I am still young.' He felt the marble tingle electrically as if it were alive. 'But I will grow big. And then everybody will see me,' he said.

He went off to hobble the mules.

Mother Beatrice came forward, breathing deeply. She leaned into the cage. The smell of the straw was strong. She shouldn't have listened. She felt guilty. She stared

78

yearningly into the virgin's face. She began an Act of Contrition. 'Hail, Mary. Full of grace . . .' and suddenly her eyes filled with tears. She was inexpressibly moved. 'Holy Mother,' she said, 'fill this young soul with serenity. Bring him to the table of thy mercy. Teach him peace . . .' and she stopped as if she had been bitten. She had disturbed something under the straw. The cold marble glistened. The militant eyes stared at her. As she looked into them with horror an odd rage of sound filled her ears. She heard the heavy tread of the Roman legions tramping about the world, the clash of arms, the hiss of arrows, the cries of the stricken. And she recoiled. She wanted to dash the marble to the ground. She caught her breath and thrust it like a spider back under the straw. And then she crossed herself and went away.

VIII

CAESAR was staring at the stars. He felt Mother Beatrice pluck his arm. 'Look,' she said excitedly. She pointed down into the darkness. The valley twinkled with specks of fire.

'I can see them,' he said.

'They are camped there.'

'All right. And we are camped here. Tomorrow will be another long haul. I want to get some sleep.'

'Come with me.' She went on tugging at him.

'Where?'

'Let us go to them. The two of us. Do an old woman an act of charity. I want you to make your peace with them,' she said.

'Why would I want to do that?'

Sister Ursula said in a tremulous voice, 'It would please God.'

'It wouldn't please me.'

Maria stood over him. 'Get up,' she said belligerently. 'Do as you are told. Why can't you show a nicer spirit? You're always fighting somebody. Try a little love for a change.'

He was amazed. 'Love that fat Brazzolo?'

'The Sisters are ordering you to love him,' Maria said irritably.

'It doesn't make sense. He doesn't love me. Why should I love him?'

'Will you stop arguing?'

'Come,' Mother Beatrice begged. 'For my sake. For the sake of your immortal soul. He is a good man. He is suffering great strain. Show him affection. Believe in the goodness of human nature. He will respond.'

'You know how? He will kick me.'

'You will no doubt deserve it,' Maria said.

'All right.' Caesar sighed. He got up. He had some private reservations about human nature. He also had a few about his enemy, Major-General Brazzolo. He looked at the three entreating feminine faces and thought: I will try. He still couldn't see what good it would do his immortal soul.

He stared down into the darkness. The valley was steep. The going would be rough. 'You are a weak old woman,' he said to Mother Beatrice. 'If you like I will go myself.'

'No,' she said hastily. She obviously didn't trust the niceness of his spirit. 'I will go with you. I am stronger than you think.'

He brought the donkeys across. Numbers One and Two snickered. They were hungry. He had seen them ride the donkeys before. 'Could they come with us?' he asked Mother Beatrice. 'They might find something to eat on the way.' She beamed. He was already showing signs of charity. He released the chimpanzees from the cage. He heaved Mother Beatrice up on to Castor's back. He mounted Pollux. The chimpanzees slipped up behind them. They rode pillion like circus artistes.

The donkeys picked their way delicately down the dark slope. Sister Ursula watched them depart with her heart in her mouth. It was like something out of a medieval tapestry: the pilgrims were on their way. She caught a last glimpse of the boy bobbing ludicrously on the donkey with a chimpanzee clinging to his back. That wasn't quite so medieval. 'And watch your tongue,' Maria shouted warningly after Caesar.

He called back, 'Yours isn't exactly a good example.'

And then they were gone. Sister Ursula felt suddenly lonely with Maria and two militant mules. She pressed her crucifix. Heaven will give them a successful mission, she thought.

Caesar fixed his eyes on the twinkling fires. They glittered like beads in the base of the valley. It was a distressing descent. He heard Mother Beatrice gasp. He wondered curiously why an old woman, with so little time left, should be frightened. He had a whole eternity of life in front of him and he wasn't frightened at all. They stopped now and again to let the chimpanzees search for food. There was nothing but rock. They looked disappointed. It wasn't worth coming along.

And then the smell of smoke was in their nostrils; the donkeys' hooves clattered daintily down to the verge. A soldier saw the white glimmer of Mother Beatrice's head-dress in the darkness. He turned the headlamps of a truck full on them. He crossed himself convulsively. He was a simple man. He had seen pictures like this in church: the women with the apostles riding asses into Jerusalem. The whole detachment rose. Major-General Brazzolo stared. He was a reasonably devout man. He found the sight of Mother Beatrice on the donkey biblical, too. Then he saw Caesar. And it stopped being biblical to him. He felt a small hot surge of rage.

'Stay where you are, boy,' Sergeant Naso said softly to Caesar. 'Where I can see you. I don't trust you out of my sight.'

'It's all right. I don't mean any harm.'

'You've done enough. I will break your kneecaps if you do any more.'

Mother Beatrice got down. She adjusted her habit. 'Major-general,' she started . . .

'Take that boy away,' Major-General Brazzolo said.

'He has come to make his peace with you.'

Major-General Brazzolo considered this remarkable statement. It was unbelievable. He said in a thick insulted voice, 'You are addressing an officer of field rank. That ragamuffin wishes to make his peace with *me*?'

'He is young.'

'What has that got to do with it. Do you know what damage he has done?'

She shrugged. 'He feels a certain sense of his importance . . .'

'He isn't important at all,' the major-general cried. 'He is a monster of arrogance. Look at him. An urchin. How old is he? He doesn't even shave. He needs a father's strap . . .'

'There is no father.'

'I will be glad to do it for him,' the major-general said. 'Come here.' He was incensed. 'Look.' He was showing her the wounded tank-transport. The sides of the vehicle were ripped. The great gun had suffered a bang from the rock. The anti-flash muzzle was bent. The major-general showed her trucks dented by the gully that had trapped them. It had been a nightmare backing out. 'I could charge that boy with wilful destruction of army property under Section Ten of the Military Act . . .'

'Are you going to?'

'No.' The major-general sighed frustratedly. 'It would make a laughing-stock of me,' he said.

'Forgive him.'

'Take him away. My patience is exhausted.'

Caesar's patience was almost exhausted, too. He looked calculatingly at the ruin he had wrought: let him watch out, he thought. This is nothing to what I shall do before I am done.

He got down off Pollux. The chimpanzees got down, too.

'There is so much pain and misery about us,' Mother Beatrice said. 'Nature has done something terrible. We are all in dire distress. We must help each other on our way.'

'You are welcome to come with us. That boy will lead you into trouble.'

83

'I do not think so.' Mother Beatrice knew that God had brought her to him. 'I have a belief in him,' she said.

'What do you want me to do?'

'What would you do if he were your son?'

The question hurt the major-general. He had no son. He had three daughters. They weren't a good substitute. He stared queerly at the boy's self-possessed face. Something creaked in him. He would never have confessed that he yearned to have a son like that.

He relented. He was about to say, 'Very well. He is forgiven . . .' when one of the donkeys skipped. It began a rhythmic trot. There was a radio in a truck pouring out music. It was like the smell of opium to an addict. Both donkeys began suddenly to gambol. They twirled and twisted about the major-general.

The chimpanzees grew excited. They were used to joining in the act. They clutched the major-general friendlily. He felt the hairy arms of one of them wrapped about his trousers, and the other clawing up his back. He was offended beyond endurance. He was overrun by chattering apes and dancing donkeys, and he heard the men laugh. His rage returned. 'For God's sake,' Sergeant Naso said. It shocked him. He stared with alarm at Lieutenant Arnolfo and they drove the chimpanzees off. The donkeys went on dancing. They were like clockwork toys that would go on until the movement ran down.

'Get him away,' the major-general said. Caesar had done nothing. But the major-general hated him.

'Yes.' Mother Beatrice grew nervous. Anything she said would only make the situation worse. 'Come.' She motioned to Caesar. She was afraid to get on the donkey until it was quite still.

'I told you it was a waste of time. I know how to deal with him.'

'Please, my son. No more of that,' she begged.

The major-general said, 'If he is not out of this camp in one minute . . .'

'Go on, boy,' Sergeant Naso said. 'Get out of here while you are safe.'

'The man is mad. He isn't fit to hold a command.'

'That will do,' Lieutenant Arnolfo warned Caesar. 'You have said enough.'

They walked the donkeys up the slope until the fascination of the music had worn off. Caesar helped Mother Beatrice up. The chimpanzees mounted pillion. They climbed on.

Sister Ursula was waiting for them at the top. 'Everything went well?' she asked anxiously.

Everything had gone horribly. Mother Beatrice didn't want to disappoint her. She looked reflectively at Caesar. 'He is learning the lesson that comes hardest to the young.'

Caesar wondered what it was.

'Self-discipline,' she said.

He thought about this as he went to sleep. She is a hopelessly naïve woman, but she could be right. Discipline is the anvil on which one hammers oneself into steel. I will hammer myself into a hard blade. And then I will let that fat Brazzolo feel the edge of it, he thought.

Mother Beatrice lay watching the stars. Her feelings were mixed. If heaven hadn't chosen her vocation for her – if she had been permitted motherhood – it might have been a holy mission to raise a child for God. She felt genuinely sorry for Caesar. She thought he'd tried hard to placate the major-general. He hadn't. She had been given this tender young soul to mould. In fact, he was about as malleable as rock. She felt sorry for Major-General Brazzolo, too. The recollection of the two donkeys dancing about him as if he were a maypole made her giggle. It was wicked. She thought of the chimpanzees wrapped about him familiarly, one on his back, one round his legs. And her giggles grew worse. She was ashamed of herself. She choked them down. She said a decade on her Rosary and three Hail Marys as a penance. And then she turned over and went to sleep.

IX

SHE was being suffocated. She knew towards the end of the
dream that that was exactly what it was, but it was so real,
so full of torment, that the effort of waking up made the
sweat pour down her face. It was a small stone on her chest.
It was no bigger than a melon. But its weight was frightful,
and it was getting bigger and bigger all the time. It had a
face. It was familiar to her. She had seen it in museums. It
had a tongue, too. It spoke to her. It was in antique Latin.
Mother Beatrice understood Latin, having had a religious
education. It was a voice out of a two-thousand-year-old
grave.

'The boy is mine,' it said. 'He belongs to me. I have lain
in the earth all these centuries. Now I am awake. And I am
going to give him a little of my life.'

By straining her neck she could look straight into the cool
marble eyes. They made her shiver.

'No,' she said. 'He belongs to God.'

'That's right,' the head said. 'I am the divine Caesar.
I am God.'

Mother Beatrice could see the radiance of heaven in the
dream. There was the swirl of the drapery of angels. She
felt strengthened. 'Anti-Christ,' she said chokingly to the
head.

It seemed a little surprised. It was a handsome face. The
sculptor had idealized the features. Nobody makes emperors
look ugly. The brow was broad. The hair grew low on it
in a boyish fringe. But this was no boy. The lips had an
arrogant Greek curl. The sculptor, in fact, was a Greek.

He had modelled Big Julius on Alexander. 'Anti-who?' Big Julius asked. 'Some Egyptian general? I never heard of him. I must have been before his time.'

Mother Beatrice tried to mutter a few words of exorcism. She kept her eyes fixed on the angels.

'I am going to shape that boy,' Big Julius said. 'He's good metal.'

'I beg of you. Let him be.'

'Don't be silly. I shall tell him the mistakes I made so that he won't repeat them. We will fight a few wars together. It should be fun,' Big Julius said.

And all the time he was crushing down on Mother Beatrice's bosom.

'I shall teach him peace,' she gasped. 'In the name of God.'

'We seem to be talking at cross-purposes,' Big Julius said. 'I am God. And I am a man of war.'

'God is love.'

'I once knew a goddess of love.' The stone eyes glistened. 'Her name was Cleopatra. She nearly brought me to a bad end. That is another thing I shall teach him. How to handle women.'

He was now as heavy as a mountain. She struggled frantically for breath.

'Have pity on him. He is young.'

'I know,' Big Julius chuckled. 'Just give me the boy while he's impressionable. Then you can have the man.'

Mother Beatrice felt that she had to make one last effort. 'I shall save him from you,' she burst out, and it woke her. Sister Ursula was rubbing her hands.

'What is it?' she asked anxiously.

'Nothing. It's all right.' Mother Beatrice licked her lips. 'The ground is hard.'

She looked round for the boy. He was blowing up the fire. The dawn was coming over the peaks like a razor edge. It was a cold morning. 'You had a bad dream,' Caesar said.

'Yes.' She couldn't take her eyes off him. He would never know how bad.

'Here.' He gave her a cup of hot water. 'No breakfast. There's just enough for one more meal.'

'You know best, my son.'

'That's right.' He had resumed the unconscious leadership. 'Now let's move.'

'Five minutes? Just to . . .?'

'Make it a three-minute prayer. And while you're at it remind God that we're running out of food.'

The apes were rattling the bars. They were famished. The mules sniffled. Caesar slapped their haunches. 'You know what they say,' he told them. 'An empty belly makes a sharp mind.' He hitched them up. Mother Beatrice seemed to want to ride with him. He helped her on to the cage.

It was still too dark to see the convoy in the valley. There was a haze that might have been cooking fires. 'Hup,' he said to the mules. Their hollow intestines were as liquid as fountains. They clopped on.

What, Mother Beatrice wondered with astonishment, makes this eruptive un-Italian boy so sure of himself? He seemed to revel in the challenge. He was as resilient as a bamboo shoot. She wished she could communicate with him better. Fifty years lay between them. Then she thought cheerfully: but there are two thousand between him and that stone pagan. Meaning Big Julius. Even thinking of him made her shiver again.

There was a sound like coffee grinding in a mill. It was the convoy passing below. The rising sun glittered on the tank-transports frosted with dew. The tyres thudded. The staff-car, like a flea leading great bugs, wound ahead. Heaven give them a safe passage, Mother Beatrice thought. She was filled with compassion. She glanced at Caesar. He was grinning. There was no compassion on his face at all.

She wondered what was amusing him. She heard shouts

far down. There was a sporadic iron clatter. It was like a minor bombardment. Puffs of dust were bursting like shells on the hulls of the tanks and she couldn't understand what was causing it: until she saw the ripping trail of rocks down the slope.

She couldn't believe her eyes. She froze with fear. Then with moral outrage. Caesar was edging the mules calculatedly over to the verge. The crunching wheels dislodged the rocks that fringed it and they went bouncing, each with an attendant avalanche, below. He was literally aiming them like missiles. It was very dangerous. Mother Beatrice shuddered. She heard Maria call out from the rear cage, 'What are you doing? Are you mad?' and Caesar chuckled, 'Keep your eyes shut. And sit still.'

'Stop it.' Mother Beatrice found her tongue.

He ignored her.

'Stop it,' she cried again. 'Let them be.'

He watched her amusedly. 'No.'

He guided the cage precariously towards the edge, and this time even the hardened mules bleated with fear. The rocks began a thunderous descent. Mother Beatrice watched them arrive on their targets with hypnotic horror. Iron banged. The dust spurted. The man were leaning angrily out of the cabs.

'Why are you harassing them?'

'Why not? It could be the last chance. We may never see them again.'

'Have you no charity in you?' It was wrung out of her. She was trembling with rage.

'Not for them.'

'You are wicked.'

'Am I?' The last chance was going. A wheel of the cage hung for a heart-stopping moment in the air: the mules whined piteously. The convoy went skittering on like a dinosaur escaping a gad-fly. A rock clanged on the staff-car.

90

Mother Beatrice saw Major-General Brazzolo brandish his fists. Then the line of armour was gone, leaving the valley hazed with fumes; and the gritty roar of the exhausts was lost in the hollow corridors of the mountains.

For about four minutes Mother Beatrice had been horribly scared. Fear to her was a condition that implied lack of faith in God. She would never have thought herself capable of it. She felt her headband, which was chafing her neck. It was wet with sweat. It was filthy, too. It disgusted her. That wasn't Caesar's fault, of course. Her mind went searching off for the furious phrases of her novicehood: this is a child of Beelzebub, she thought. She could smell the mules. They were unsavoury with sweat and saliva. They were capable of stark horror, too.

She heard Caesar chuckle. She wanted to hit him. She knew that she was about to commit three distinct and probably unforgivable sins: the sins of intolerance, haste and unkindness.

And she was too convulsed to care.

'Why are you laughing?' she demanded.

'I thought it was funny.'

She almost blazed. '*Funny?*'

'Didn't you see fat Brazzolo jump?'

'I saw you persecute him. It was cruel.'

He stopped twinkling. His face closed up like a camera iris. He gave her a cold look. He was thinking: this is a dried-up old woman who has withdrawn from the battle of life. She shelters behind something veiled called God. I cannot see behind veils. I like to look a thing straight in the face. I have looked at God, back in the cage there, and all I know is that he has to depend on my quick brain to get him home.

Mother Beatrice was thinking: this is a devil of a boy. I am wasting my time on him. He has the malignant wit of Satan. Why am I trying to redeem him? She knew that she

91

was increasing the burden of her sin every moment by even thinking such things.

Worse still – much much worse – she was in danger of losing her head.

She waited for him to say something. All he said was 'Hup' to the mules.

'Tell me that you are sorry,' she said harshly.

'No.'

Her voice rose. 'Tell me at least that you are . . .'

'I don't want to argue with you. You're getting excited,' he said.

And she was. She tugged at her neckband. He is obdurate, she thought. Mother Beatrice had run her little convent in the mountains rather like a martinet. The Sisters were as nervous of her as Armageddon. Nobody, not even the pertest novice, had spoken to her like that for thirty years.

And she cried out, 'Is it possible that you are evil?'

For that remark alone she would say limitless Our Fathers and Hail Marys. She wondered agonizedly: what am I saying?

'I don't know,' he said indifferently. 'What do you think?'

'Cannot you show your brothers kindness?'

'I've told you six times. I don't have any brothers. I just have me. Caesar no-name.'

The mules were lagging. She was shocked to see him do something revolting to their rumps with a stick. It galvanized them.

'Boy!'

He looked her over. He wasn't frightened of her at all.

'Why are you shouting?'

'You have a precious soul . . .'

'It can look after itself. I'm too busy looking after us. I have an empty stomach to fill. *Four* empty stomachs,' he said pointedly, looking at her habit in the region of her belly. 'Let me get on with my job.'

'Mine is the care of your spiritual . . .'

'Who told you that?'

It staggered her.

'In God's name,' she burst out. 'Be humble.'

She wasn't being very humble. And he knew it. He looked at her disdainfully.

'No. I won't,' he said.

She felt suddenly short of breath. She didn't know what to say.

'It's a world of wolves and sheep. The wolves eat. The sheep get clipped,' he said. He went on seriously, 'You're a woman. It's right for you to be humble.' It was a startling revelation of masculinity from a boy of twelve. 'I am a man. And I am not going to be humble. Not for anybody. I am going to hold my head up. And look everybody in the face.'

Mother Beatrice began to be quite frightened of him.

She wondered why he was chuckling. 'Did you know that I can read?'

'You can?' she said faintly. She wondered what was coming next.

'Have you ever heard of Job?'

'Yes.' She licked her lips.

'I've read him,' Caesar said. He began suddenly to declaim, '"He saith among the trumpets, Ha ha! And he smelleth the battle far off, the thunder of the captains, and the shouting." Well, I'm going to smell a few battles and shout and thunder like those captains,' Caesar said.

The devil could always quote scripture to suit his purpose. This is Big Julius talking with his tongue, Mother Beatrice thought.

'Remember.' She fumbled for Holy Writ. It was a mistake. 'The meek shall inherit the earth.'

He grinned. He'd heard that, too. Standing like an eavesdropper in the door of the church, listening to the priest. Priest Quick-With-His-Hands.

93

'Like Luigi Pirelli?' he asked.

'Who is Luigi Pirelli?' She was getting terribly confused.

'He inherited most of the village of Lorenzo of the Angels. By lending at eight and a half per cent. And foreclosing fast. Not by being meek.'

It was only just short of blasphemy. And Mother Beatrice froze.

'Stop,' she cried. She snatched at his hands. 'Let me down.'

'What's the matter with you?'

'I want to get off.'

'If you'll wait a minute . . .'

'No.' She dragged the reins from his hands. The mules swerved. The nearside wheel rode over a boulder. She heard a crunch. The cage began to ride with a queer see-saw motion. Caesar jumped down to look at the wheel. It was bent.

'All right,' he said flatly to Mother Beatrice. 'Get down.'

She was shocked by the intensity of her emotion. 'What have I done?'

'Enough.' She got down. Sister Ursula and Maria had hurried over. 'Do that again,' Caesar said brutally, 'and you can take God and walk the rest of the way.'

'I am sorry.'

Mother Beatrice couldn't catch her breath. She walked away. Sister Ursula ran after her, wringing her hands.

'What did he say to you?'

'Nothing. The boy is abandoned.'

'No, no,' Sister Ursula cried. 'How can he be? At his age?'

'He is as pagan as . . .' Mother Beatrice was going to say 'Big Julius' but she couldn't bear to mention his name.

'We must have patience.'

'I am too old for it.'

'Heaven has infinite patience.'

'Yes.' Mother Beatrice stopped trembling. She looked

into Sister Ursula's withered-apple face. She found strength. 'We shall redeem him yet,' she said.

'You're absolutely maddening,' Maria was whispering angrily to Caesar. 'Can't you behave yourself?'

Caesar had had almost enough. He said ungallantly, 'Hold your tongue.'

'Is that how you address a lady?'

'What lady? You're a fairground-man's daughter.'

She drew herself up with dignity. 'Look what you've done to the wheel.'

'I didn't do it.'

'You have inconvenienced God. He must be very angry with you. You know that he is in a hurry to get to Rome.'

'He doesn't help much, does he?'

'Blasphemer,' she said, with the insufferable holiness of a believer.

'You'd better be careful.'

'You will burn when you die,' she said. But he'd stopped listening. He was staring back at the rear cage with a tight, screwed-up expression.

Mother Beatrice was leaning into the straw. She fumbled beneath it. She found the marble head. She stared at it with fascinated horror. She was tempted to dash it to the ground. And she stood there, trembling with indecision, feeling the cold stone literally burn her hands. 'Guide me, holy mother,' she said yearningly to the virgin. 'Show me . . .' but it was too late. She felt a stir behind her. Caesar was watching her.

She put it down. She was as shocked as if she had been found pilfering the poor-box. 'It's all right,' she said guiltily. He was angry. He brushed past her and covered it ostentatiously with straw. She looked gratefully at the virgin. She was glad she hadn't succumbed to the temptation. There are other ways to his salvation, she thought.

When he went back she was already perched on the cage. He was surprised that she would still want to sit with him.

He squatted to take another look at the wheel. He found himself staring straight into the faces of Numbers One and Two through the bars. It was the axle that was bent. It would probably ride: but ludicrously. Still, it was no more ludicrous than travelling over the roof of Italy with two chimpanzees in a cage. And a pair of pirouetting donkeys. *And* God in the back.

He chuckled. His good humour returned.

He climbed up. Mother Beatrice wondered why he was grinning. He snapped the mules into motion. The cage rolled on lop-sidedly, see-saw fashion. To Maria, watching incredulously from the back, it looked like a straw bobbing on the waves. It reminded her nostalgically of the ponies on the merry-go-round.

Sister Ursula it merely made giddy. She looked away.

'You are angry with me,' Mother Beatrice said to Caesar.

'I was.' He bent to peer at Numbers One and Two. He hoped they wouldn't be sea-sick. 'I have forgiven you,' he said.

'Thank you.'

'You see that rosary of yours?' She was plucking at it absently.

'Yes?'

'It means something to you?'

'Everything.'

'That is what Big Julius means to me. We all have to have something. He is my rosary.'

Mother Beatrice's mouth opened with revulsion. She shut it. The motion of the cage was making her stomach very uneasy.

She was aware of a hollow sound. It was like peas rattling in a jug. It stopped. Then came again. It groaned out of the very belly of the earth. Above the squeak and clatter of the cage she seemed to feel a tremor. And for no apparent reason, with a squeal, the mules shied. The two donkeys trembled.

They tried to stop, but the rope attaching them to the cage dragged them on. And then again it happened. A grunt and a belch from the mountain: and there was the thunder of avalanching rocks from the tops.

Caesar watched it grimly. He had felt the tremor, too. It was starting again.

He jabbed at the mules. They didn't want to go on. He kicked cruelly at their rumps. He could hear them snorting. They plodded on. The chimpanzees plucked with terror at the bars of the cage. He could hear their almost-human moans. He was afraid of the showering rocks, plunging like loosened snow from the heights.

He looked humourlessly at Mother Beatrice. He jerked his head back. 'Can't you get him to stop it?'

She knew whom he meant.

'It will pass.' She hoped so. She wasn't afraid for herself. She had lived most of her life. For this boy she just wanted God to live on.

'Why does he do it?'

'There are many things beyond our small comprehension,' Mother Beatrice said. There were quite a few things beyond hers. She was prepared to abide in patience until her earthly release, when all things would be revealed. 'Must we understand everything?'

'Yes,' Caesar said. She was surprised by his passion. 'I have to know everything. If I have to die before I have even begun to live, I want to know why.'

She started to say, 'As you grow older . . .' but he interrupted her almost as soon as she opened her mouth.

'Do you think I am going to?'

She stared with shock into the serious young face. The harshness of the question upset her: it was monstrous to think of him not growing up.

'Yes.'

'Is that a promise?'

'My son . . .'

'Why don't you go back and ask him? You're in business with him.'

'Faith is better.'

He grinned at her ironically. The sky had the sultry blaze it had had the day of the first shocks: standing in the dock, wondering why the animals were so quiet. The heat seemed to scrape like sandpaper on his neck. He draped his handkerchief cowl-fashion about his head. Little drops of sweat glistened oilily on his arms. He blinked up at the silent peaks. The rocks had stopped falling. Every sound, the squeak of the bent axle, the rattle of the cage hup-hupping on it comically, the dry crunch of the wheels, the plop of the mules' hooves, the nervous whinny of the donkeys, was magnified. A few heavy birds had come out of their eyries: they were wheeling uneasily in the sky as if their homes were no longer safe. And they weren't.

He felt the splintering quiver: the mules reared. They bleated. Castor and Pollux dragged back at the cage. Caesar lashed out at them. The mountain slopes loosened again. They poured rubble like waterfalls. They crashed ahead. They could take us away like straws, he thought.

He said angrily to Mother Beatrice, jerking his head back, 'Does it give him pleasure?'

She didn't answer.

'You think maybe he's a little young? You think he'll learn to give up these practical jokes when he grows up?'

Mother Beatrice turned to stare at Sister Ursula. She wished there was someone to take the brunt of this terrible interrogation as well as herself.

She had had to retire behind her head-dress from the glare of the sun. She was suffocating inside it. She heard something thump up in the peaks. She saw one of them dissolve. There had been a crag like a broken thumb: and then it wasn't there at all. The skin of the mountain peeled off. She heard the fragments crash into some hidden gully.

A dark corner of her mind – the one that sometimes confessed to doubts – suddenly felt like Caesar about heavenly practical jokes. These violent convulsions belonged more to the old sporting gods: Zeus grinning down from the clouds as he spat out volcanoes, Apollo flinging thunderbolts like an exultant athlete from the sky.

To have even been *capable* of thinking such things made her sweat. She looked frantically round for Sister Ursula. She needed her. They recharged each other's faith.

She was in the state of natural terror that was ready to anticipate what happened next. The earth billowed like a mattress. The road tilted. Somebody had his thumb under it: probably Zeus. He was laughing. The mules' hooves slithered for grip. And with her eyes closed, shrinking behind her head-dress, Mother Beatrice felt the two cages, one bearing the precious burden of God, the other the moaning apes, rolling helplessly down the tilt.

X

MAJOR-GENERAL BRAZZOLO was suffering in the staff-car. The heat was liquefying his fat. It gushed from under his cap, drenching his shirt. He was a fastidious man. And his condition disgusted him. I am stewing in my own gravy, he thought.

He peered into the mirror. He could see the snake of the convoy thudding unstoppably behind. They had made quite a respectable distance. Perhaps – he allowed himself the hope – they might even reach Naples tomorrow night? It should have encouraged him. And for some deep instinctive reason it didn't. He felt a brooding sense of ill-omen.

There is a raven sitting on my shoulder, he thought.

He glanced at Luigi Pirelli sitting at his side. He had begun to detest him. The man talked incessantly. Before his mouth opened his hands were already shaping the words like putty. He smelled of garlic. Why? Nobody else in the convoy smelled of garlic. There had been no food for three days remotely flavoured with it. And the staff-car smelled like a salami factory. The major-general looked into the mirror at the Pirelli daughter sitting behind. He thought with distaste: how ill-favoured she is. He wished he hadn't been so ready to accept them as passengers.

He stared through the rear window. He could see Sergeant Naso in the cab of the truck behind. He was smoking. He looked relaxed. The major-general felt quite oddly unrelaxed.

Then something strange happened. He couldn't feel anything through the judder of the wheel. But he had had a distinct sense of vibration. For an instant his vision blurred. The steep slopes seemed to go out of focus. He rubbed his tired eyes. They were swimmy from the endless twisting of the road. It was probably nervous exhaustion. He had moved his head. He found himself staring into the mirror straight at Luigi Pirelli's wife, sitting immediately behind. The queer basilisk glare was fixed on the back of his neck. The tic jumped convulsively.

The major-general thought: there is nothing wrong with my eyes. And it isn't a raven sitting on my shoulder. It is the woman sitting behind me. She has the evil eye.

Major-General Brazzolo had been educated at Pisa technical school. He had studied electronics at Bologna University. He read Plato and Bertrand Russell: he believed in modern rational philosophy. He professed a kind of scientific Christianity that wasn't really Christianity at all. He was a well-adjusted agnostic. And at heart – like all Italians – he was as impressionable as a Cherokee Indian. Occasionally his mathematical eye winced as it passed over the number thirteen. He knew it was something unscientific to do with the Last Supper, which had no significance to him. And still he winced.

He moved his head so that he shouldn't have to look into the twittering eye. He could still feel it on the back of his neck.

I do not know how long I can suffer this, he thought.

The road corkscrewed on through the stony corridors of the mountains like a frizzled hair. He tugged at his collar. It was wet with sweat. He looked up at the vast silent stony ledges. Were they quite silent? He saw a rock-fall high, high up. It threshed like a torrent down the stark slopes. He couldn't hear anything above the coarse judder of the road. But again – this time startlingly – there was that swimmy sensation. The feeling that there had been a great physical shudder. This was the moment that Caesar and Mother

Beatrice, crawling up on the top like invisible flies, had felt the first real splintering quiver: with the mules dragging and bleating. Something must have communicated itself to Sergeant Naso. The major-general thought he had stiffened in the cab of the truck. He had shoved his head out. He looked like a troubled animal.

I am troubled, too, the major-general thought, but differently. I have this gorgon behind me, drilling malevolently into the back of my neck.

He felt the staff-car swerve: and scrape the verge. He gasped. He looked down for a petrifying instant into yawning depths. He leapt with sweat. He had been day-dreaming. He was desperately tired. He looked round quickly at Luigi Pirelli's wife. The dreadful eye was still twittering. He put out his hand to signal: stop. He saw hands in every vehicle repeat the signal. The convoy slowed down at the verge. Then stopped.

The major-general got out. Lieutenant Arnolfo approached from the rear. His eyes said curiously: everything is going well. What is wrong?

The major-general drew him out of earshot and said huskily, 'Get them out of my car. I have had enough.'

'Major-general. There is a psychological situation . . .'

'There's one for me, too. I am human. I cannot suffer that woman behind me any longer.'

'She is upsetting you?'

'Of course she is upsetting me.'

'I will tell her to stop talking . . .'

'She isn't talking. She is just looking at me.'

'Ah.' Lieutenant Arnolfo gave him an odd look. He sighed.

He was a little surprised. Field-officers of the Italian army weren't expected to be that susceptible. And this was a scientific officer, too. It was irrational. Lieutenant Arnolfo also read Plato, if not Bertrand Russell. He was a fundamentalist. This sort of fetish-nonsense was undignified. He walked over to the staff-car. He glanced inside. Luigi Pirelli's wife looked full at him. He felt his stomach move. It was irrational, too. He was also an Italian. He went back to the major-general and said, 'What do you wish me to do?'

'Tell Sergeant Naso to make room for them in one of the trucks.'

'Major-general. With all respect . . .'

'It is an order. Orders are meant to be obeyed.'

'I will ask the sergeant . . .'

'Don't ask him. *Tell* him.'

'Of course.' The men had climbed out of the cabs. They pretended to be stretching. There was an empty obduracy in their expressions. They had guessed the trend of the conversation. Sergeant Naso was standing near by. Just near enough to satisfy his curiosity. But not near enough to be involved. The lieutenant went across to him and said, bluntly, 'You heard?'

'I heard.'

'Well?'

'Lieutenant. If I may be frank.' The lieutenant hoped he wasn't going to carry frankness to the point of insubordination. 'We understand each other. We are civilized animals. Do not push the men too far. They are scared. We are in an unpredictable situation. Anything can happen. We may not come out of this alive. An officer should not order his men,' the sergeant said, glancing woodenly at the major-general, 'to do what he would not do himself.'

'To ask them to make room for a family in a truck? It is a Christian act . . .'

'They are not Christians. They are Neapolitans. They are almost as superstitious as Sicilians,' the sergeant said cheerfully, 'of whom I am one.'

'This is absurd.'

'I know. I would not carry that woman for anything. If

I were a pregnant woman she would curdle my milk. She
has the evil eye.'

'You are a soldier. How can you be such a primitive?'

'If I weren't a primitive would I be a soldier? I would be
in the Mafia. I would earn a good living as a fixer.' The
sergeant lowered his voice. 'Be discreet. Tell the good
major-general to go to hell.'

'How do you do that discreetly?'

'I don't know. That is why you are an officer, and I am
just a sergeant.'

'You're not helping much.'

'At this particular moment,' Sergeant Naso said coolly,
'I am concentrating chiefly on helping myself.' He looked
up at the molten sky. The great peaks simmered. The silence
was uncanny. 'I do not like the look of it. I fought in two
wars. I was in Abyssinia. I was in Greece. And you know
what this is like? Zero hour. Ten seconds before the
bombardment.'

'I am ashamed of you.'

'I lived through both wars. I am going to live through
this one, too,' the sergeant said.

The major-general waited impatiently. He tore open his
shirt. He found it hard to breathe. He, too, looked up at the
burning shield of the sky. Why was it so quiet? A few birds
wheeled uneasily. Luigi Pirelli got out of the car and came
across. His fingers were weaving while he was still walking.
They made the pulsating judder of the combustion engine.
'Has the motor broken down?' Then a big scoop to suggest
the question mark. 'What is holding us up?'

The major-general was tempted to say: you are. He turned
away. The salami smell was strong.

'You are a civilian passenger. It is not for you to ask
questions,' he said.

'It is distressing my wife.'

The major-general avoided looking at her.

'Will you go away?'

'I pay taxes,' Luigi said. This was an exaggeration. He was by nature and avarice anti-tax. 'I am entitled to the respect of our armed forces . . .'

'*Be quiet*,' the major-general said intensely.

Something had happened. He felt a terrible nausea. He was tempted for a moment to put out his hand to steady himself. He had felt the rush of an express train – it was an absurdity in these lonely mountains – under his feet. It had shaken the earth. It only lasted a second or two. He might have thought it imagination, if he had not seen a few pebbles roll loosely and fall over the verge. He didn't hear them fall. It was too far down.

'May God help us.' Luigi trembled wildly. 'It is starting again.'

The major-general had had his eyes fixed on a crag like a crooked thumb. *Had* was the operative word – for it was no longer there. Some vast breath had puffed it off the sky-line. This was the crag Mother Beatrice had been watching. She had heard it crash into some hidden gully. It was the gully in which the major-general was standing. It was a long way up and the sound of the fracture came like a delayed shot. It was followed by a rumble. The major-general guessed that the falling peak was gathering an avalance of rock for company as it came along. He saw trees vanish. The sound grew. His eyes sighted the direction, and it seemed to be coming straight at them.

Sergeant Naso came to the same conclusion at that instant. The major-general heard him shout, 'Run,' – heard the scamper of steps as the men spread like bird-shot – and slowly his heavy limbs moved him too. He ran. He had never run so fast in his life.

He flurried the Pirelli family ahead of him. The wife shrieked as she ran. Lieutenant Arnolfo was already shepherding the few survivors of the village of Lorenzo of the

Angels. Angels, the major-general thought – if only I had angels' wings. He felt the hammer on his breath. There was a pulse bursting in his head. The rumble was now a monstrous burble of sound. It wasn't being delayed much. It was very near. The first rocks thumped on to the road, well back from the major-general, and he flung himself on his face in the shelter of the cliff.

Then the road leapt like a mattress under his belly. He felt the massive shock of crashing stone. He felt splinters stinging his head. Something thudded solidly on his back. Then dust descended on him and he choked and choked. The sound rushed on, then faded like a gramophone record running down. It was comparatively quiet. He got up, spat the dust out of his mouth, felt himself for blood – there was a graze from a flying splinter on his hand – and rubbed his eyes.

He could see two trucks beyond the mound of rock. They were the only vehicles to be seen. They were dented. One sagged like a cripple on broken springs. He could see the muzzle of a solitary gun twisted vengefully up at the mountain out of a hillock of rubble – but the transports were gone. The section of the road had gone with them. There was the hissing crackle of fire somewhere over the verge – a sudden sharp explosion: and more fire. He walked near, climbing over shattered stone. He looked down into the valley. He saw a turret or two, bent like tin toys that a bored child had smashed in a rage. The fuel-bowser burned furiously. There was a litter of broken tank-treads and scattered wheels. The chassis of a transport lay upside down. The rest were decently covered.

The avalanche had buried them, like a tidy murderer concealing a crime.

The major-general saw Sergeant Naso counting heads. He walked on a little way. He discovered his staff-car flattened under rock. A wheel, torn loose, still revolved with a tinny whirr. It brought the enormity of the shock closer. He looked vacantly at a tear in his sleeve. He was filthy. He sucked the blood off his hand. Lieutenant Arnolfo watched him wearily. The men who had been counted sat down.

Sergeant Naso came up. He looked grim.

'Two gone,' he said. 'Pacelli and Veroni. The rest are all right.'

The major-general flinched. 'You are sure they are not under the . . . ?'

'I saw them go over with the stuff,' the sergeant said.

'It is bad.'

'Yes.'

The sergeant waited for the major-general to be practical. They had problems. He'd fought in Abyssinia and Greece and never trembled like this. The major-general beckoned him over to the trucks. He checked the gauges. There wasn't enough fuel for six kilometres. The rest burned below. He shrugged negatively.

The major-general looked into the back of the trucks. They contained radar-gear. It was a pity. You couldn't eat it. The ration trucks also burned below.

He looked at Sergeant Naso and said softly, 'What rations do they carry?' He didn't want the men to hear.

Sergeant Naso stared back. A motorized unit was lazy. It ate off its wheels.

The major-general said painfully, 'Soldiers are supposed to carry enough on manoeuvres for . . .'

'Yes.' The sergeant shrugged again. It was the Italian army. He said cruelly, 'This is a technical detachment. They are not the Coldstream Guards.'

'Throw these trucks over. They contain secret equipment. We cannot leave them here.'

The sergeant looked at them. It was valuable stuff. One panelful of instruments would have bought him a fat annuity. It was the wastage of the army. 'Yes, major-general.'

He started up one of the trucks and steered it over the verge. It shattered below. The other had a bent chassis. Nothing would shift it. Lieutenant Arnolfo threw the loose equipment over the cliff.

'Now march,' the major-general said.

'Up on your feet. And march,' the sergeant said to the men. They were still numb with shock. They looked at him emptily. His tone wasn't affable any more. He kicked one of them erect. The rest stood. They had received the message. They formed up into a vaguely military column and trudged off along the road.

Mother Beatrice found herself looking down beyond the verge into depths that made her head swim. She heard Maria scream and thought broken-heartedly: if only I could be with the child. She was a passionate believer in the power of prayer. She looked up, as much to tear her eyes from the sickening depths, as to seek comfort in heaven. The road didn't stop tilting: Zeus was still laughing. The road began to splinter like glass. There was the dimming rumble of thundering rock. It was Zeus' last laugh.

He had transferred his amusement elsewhere. The crag had just crashed into that hidden gully. He had seen it sweep the convoy away.

The mules pawed and pounded like trick-cyclists at the fragmented road. They were stupid animals; but they realized that they were attached to the cages. Death is supposed to concentrate the mind wonderfully. Where the cages went, they went too. It concentrated their minds. They snorted. One wheel hung for a little interval over the edge. It skidded. Caesar bent to look at it. It was the one with the skewed axle. He thought humorously, we can spare it.

His mind was divided into two clear parts. One was grappling with the problem of gravity: the other was fixed on himself. He was glad to note that he wasn't frightened. He was getting a kind of fierce excitement out of the skidding cage; the wheel tearing at the verge; the bitter gasping of the mules. Mother Beatrice stared into the boy's enraptured face. I will never understand him, she thought.

He swarmed forward on to the back of the nearside mule. He was now an animal part of the struggle, and he spat intimately into the beast's ear. 'Work,' he said to it. 'Work for your life.' It howled. What else was consuming it, but the yearning for life? The hooves slithered. The cages struggled from the edge.

Mother Beatrice thought gratefully: heaven has answered. Caesar thought: I have done it. I have tested myself in adversity and I have kept my head. He went like an acrobat over the mule's head and grabbed at its muzzle. He helped it to haul. He kicked the other under the belly. It wasn't to help it. It was an act of exultation. He grinned up at Mother Beatrice, now perched solitarily on the cage. She was frightened of him. The two cages went up the tilt and rolled on to securer ground.

Well, we are not going to die just this minute, Caesar thought. And, if I can help it, not at all.

He wiped the mules' saliva off his hands. He let them rest. Their eyes were mad.

He climbed up on to the cage and called back, 'Not to worry,' to Maria.

She wept. Men work and women weep, he thought.

He didn't say anything to Mother Beatrice. There was a curious baffled look on her face.

He was about to drive off. She put her hand yearningly on his arm. 'Should you not thank heaven?'

He looked at her with astonishment. 'What for?'

'We still live.'

'I know.' He touched his living flesh proudly. 'I saw to that.'

'My son. Only by God's grace . . .'

'No, by mine,' he said. He was getting angry. 'What did he have to do with it? Nothing. He didn't lift a finger to help.'

Sister Ursula shrank. She was still yellow from her experience. She rocked her head.

'Who jumped over the mules? I did,' Caesar said. 'Who got spat on?' He showed the sticky trace of saliva on his arm. He wore it like a medal. 'Who dragged them back? I did. Is he afraid to leave his mother? He didn't even stir out of the cage.'

It's going to be a hard battle for him, Mother Beatrice thought stubbornly. But I will never give up.

'You know what I think?' Caesar said arrogantly. He wasn't so much angry now as head-and-shoulders taller. He'd grown that much in ten seconds. 'He can't be bothered. He's like me. He's too busy growing up. He leaves every-thing to us. There are too many people. You can't watch them all. You'd have to have eyes in the back of your head. He just lets the best of us get on with the job.'

'Blasphemer,' Maria said.

Caesar stopped the mules. 'Say that again,' he warned her, 'and I will throw you head over ——' using the Italian diminutive for buttocks, 'over that cage.'

He might just be capable of it. She was a prudent young woman. She held her tongue.

Mother Beatrice had a strange vision. In her mind's eye she saw the marble head lying under the straw: she saw the lips twitch into a cold smile of approval. Anti-Christ. He is using this boy as a sounding-board. Either he has him. Or God has him. I am here to see that God has him, she thought.

Sister Ursula's lips worked nervously. She glanced up.

'You're always looking up,' Caesar said with contempt.

'Why don't you look at me? I'm the only one who can help. I have a good head. I have quick muscles. You've given me a big job to do. Let me get on with it. And don't interfere.'

He waited for them to say something. Sister Ursula trembled. Mother Beatrice stared grimly ahead.

'All right,' he said masterfully. 'Now we understand each other. Hup.' And he whipped on the mules.

I suppose I was a little brusque with them. But it was necessary, he thought. The cage trundled on. It rolled like a drunkard on its skewed wheel. He glanced at Mother Beatrice's pale, pinched face. Then at Sister Ursula. Both seemed quenched. They're too concerned with heaven. That comes afterwards. I'm concerned with life. That's here and now. He looked back at the other cage. I'm sorry, God. Tell your mother it had to be done. And incidentally, God. If you can tear your mind away from sin and holiness, and thinking profound things about the universe, you might remember that we're running out of food. It's just a reminder. You don't have much of an appetite. I have.

Mother Beatrice thought with iron patience: it will come. The fear of the Lord. The peace that passeth understanding. I will never give him up. Never, never. She hadn't become Mother-Superior by being a weak woman.

Sister Ursula thought: forgive him, Lord. He is young. To her, like the lusts of the flesh, it was almost a sin. Her own sin, of course, and it was the one that sooner or later everybody commits, was that she was too old.

He is a devil, Maria thought. But he makes me bubble inside. She giggled. She was budding into a sensual Italian woman. She was frightened of his assertive tongue. But it made her feel very warm.

The sun was sinking. Caesar glanced up. He didn't like the hot leaden look of the sky. A shredded haze was creeping across it. And low down, where he could see through the gaps in the peaks, was a hard black line.

Rain, he thought. He sniffed at the air. It isn't enough. Now we have to have rain. Well, I will meet that too. Mules have a keen sense of weather: they hate to get wet. They hadn't stopped grumbling. He thought fiercely, do you see me grumbling? and flurried them on.

It had never been a serene ride. It became even less serene now. The see-saw motion of the cage was making Mother Beatrice feel ill. She set her teeth. She would rather have died at that moment than yield to the weakness of her flesh. Caesar glanced down. A hairy arm, like that of an old seaman, protruded from the cage. The apes were strumming like mad harpists at the bars. With them it was simple hunger. Caesar leaned over and said, 'Shut up.' They ceased. Go back to making love, he thought. Castor and Pollux gazed at him pathetically. They were no longer in the mood for dancing. They were hungry, too.

He felt a quick oven puff. It raised a little dust. The sun grew dim. The gauze was slipping fast across the sky. A single hard drop stung his face. He turned to look at Maria. Her eyes said: do something about it. Or we will all get wet. She had grown to rely on him for everything: food, transport, getting God to his destination, and shelter from rain. He thought, so get wet. I am no miracle-maker. You have God down there. Miracles are his business. Mother Beatrice drew her cowl about her face. The wind and the rain came together.

They were drenched in an instant. It plastered his hair down his face.

He grinned at Mother Beatrice. 'It will pass.'

She met his eyes and said, 'Everything passes.' They didn't mean quite the same thing.

He tried to ride in the lee of the cliff. But it was fringed with rock disturbed by the shocks. The hard spatter of the rain was loosening earth; it slid like a mine-sluice down the slopes. It puddled messily about the wheels. The mules minced through it like debutantes. Caesar harried them. Mother Beatrice tried not to watch. If ever I disliked an animal, he thought, it is a mule that *acts*.

The rush of the water washed them round the bend – and they came suddenly on the village.

It was as anonymous as a corpse found on an old battle-field. Caesar would always think of it emptily as the *village-that-was*. Two thirds of it was flat. The church tilted, of course: they built churches to last. The bell leaned out of the belfry. There was the sign of an *albergo* that had been crunched away. The cottages were heaps of bricks. And it was all so terribly silent: but for the hiss of the rain that was trying to wash away the earth's guilt.

A dead dog lay in a puddle. There was sodden clothing mixed with the rubble. And there were legs in the clothing, and limp pale hands. A finger stuck up out of the bricks. It pointed vengefully at the sky. Caesar wondered who it was blaming.

Then he turned his eyes away from it and said, 'Get on,' to the mules.

Mother Beatrice watched him incredulously for a moment. Then she grabbed convulsively at his sleeve. 'Where are you going?' she cried.

'On.'

'There are people. There are things to be done . . .'

'Nobody can do anything for them. They are dead.'

'Wait.' She almost screamed. 'We must do what we can. There are final rites. A few to be buried. We cannot simply leave them.' And she gasped. The rain had messed her head-band and it clung like a rag to her neck. She stared into the boy's impassive face. The water sheeted down it. He dragged his trickling hair out of his eyes.

He ignored her. He jerked at the mules. They splashed on.

'Stop.' And this time she screamed. 'Do you hear? I order you. Stop.'

'No.'

'It is an offence against human dignity . . .'

'The dead aren't interested in dignity. They just want to be left.'

'An hour. Just an hour,' Sister Ursula shrilled agonizedly from the back . . .

'No,' he said intractably. 'We're running out of food. We can't wait. We have a long way to go.'

And he looked at Maria. For once she was neutral. She wasn't particularly agonized about death, which is a long-distance affair to the young. She was as drenched as a dunked doll. She was frightened, too: she had never seen rain like it. She couldn't catch her breath.

Mother Beatrice felt stifled. She opened her mouth. And the wind derided her by driving the rain down her throat. For the first time in her life she *hated*: and it wasn't an inanimate thing she hated. It was a boy. She was so convulsed that the sickening sin of it burned away in the back of her mind. She almost made her hand into a claw. She plucked at him.

She saw him go suddenly angry. He dragged himself free. She thought: he has a stone face. Like the one behind. He is a monster. He stared at her, thinking: these old women will kill us. They're not practical. They just want to celebrate death. I want to celebrate life. Mine. And he stopped the mules ostentatiously and got down.

He unhitched the rear cage.

'All right,' he said. 'You get them home.' He jerked his head: meaning God and his mother. 'Do what you want. You are on your own.'

'You would leave us?'

'I *am* leaving you.'

'It is wicked.'

'It is necessary to be strong. If that is wicked, all right. I am wicked. Are you going to get down? Or stay and be quiet?'

'You are not polite,' Sister Ursula said. She began to cry. Maria cried, too. Chiefly because she was so wet.

Caesar sighed. He saw Mother Beatrice's face close up. He knew that he had won a victory, but it wasn't a very exciting one because they were women and old. He preferred to beat men like fat Brazzolo. He hitched the cage up again. He said, 'No more trouble from you, either,' to the mules. They glanced back at him. They were in the depths of misery. They trundled on.

They were in a long descending gully. The wind lashed down it as through a tunnel. It ululated: Caesar heard it yowling like an unleashed animal up in the peaks. He felt the gush of water down his neck, down his back; and the outflow ripple down his bare legs. We'll be in a greener valley tomorrow, he thought. All we have to do is last out.

There was a gust that nearly unseated him. Mother Beatrice lurched.

He stared up at the almost vertical stone ledges. They had been fractured by the centuries. There were caves high up in the precipices like windows: others gaped like doors. Some would shelter bats. Some a man. And as they rounded the bend he saw a lofty cavern that would shelter six trucks.

A second gust made up his mind for him. He twisted at the mules' heads. They plodded over the loose scree, straight into the cavern, and there was a warm dark hush that was almost a blessing. Something flew out in a flurry. He gasped. He unclung himself soddenly from his seat. He got down. Mother Beatrice squelched down. Both ran water on to the age-old dust.

He looked up. The roof was high. They were well in from the rain. The wind yowled past the entrance. He felt tired, but sheltered. And hungry. He dashed the water off the mules' backs. They deserved a little tenderness. He made Castor and Pollux cosy in a corner of the cavern. There wasn't much he could do for Numbers One and Two. They looked like bundles of wet fur behind the bars. Not much he could do for God, either. Nor his mother. He let them stream.

He opened the last two cans. There was no brushwood to make a fire. But the cold spaghetti was divine. He scraped out the tin and watched the light fail. This is nice. He stripped to the skin. Sister Ursula averted her eyes. He saw Maria stare at him interestedly. He rubbed himself down and felt better. He wrung out his clothes and hung them up to dry.

Then he said, 'I'm sleepy.' Mother Beatrice shook her head. She couldn't understand how he could possibly sleep. She hadn't even eaten. She was too distressed. They all sat back against the rock, listening to the runnels of water lashing down the slope, watching it grow dark. When Mother Beatrice glanced again at Caesar he was fast asleep.

During the night the rain ate away at the unstable cliff. The earthquake had loosened the surface. It was like a pile of stones a child builds on a beach; it just needed a jar to make it topple. There were boulders poised precariously: and the rain ate away at the earth, and one great stone gave way with a jerk. It started others rolling. They went in a crashing rush down the slope. Caesar woke to hear the thunder. The whole cavern was vibrating with it. It came from over his head. He heard Maria cry out, 'What is . . . ?' but before she finished the sentence the pile of rock and rubble slid down to the base of the cliff and piled over the entrance. And it was suddenly dark and silent inside: they were sealed in.

XI

He called out after a while, 'Are we all right?' There was a last gritty rumble. Then it was finished. Mother Beatrice answered. Then Maria. Then Sister Ursula, as if torn out of her shock. The apes answered, too. He heard them moan. 'Sit still,' he said. He reached out with the elaborate care of the blind. He bumped into the cage. It was what he was looking for. He felt in his personal bundle for the matches. He had had the sense to keep them wrapped against the damp. You can't be too practical, he thought.

He struck a match. He was close to the cage. The first thing he saw in the glimmer was the startled face of Number Two. Number One clung to her. It was the correct order of seniority that the male should be Number One and the female Number Two. She reached plaintively through the bars and pressed his hand. 'It's all right,' he said. 'It's just dark. Wait for the morning and the sun'll come up.'

Mother Beatrice stared at him fixedly. He stared back. Sister Ursula's face worked as if she still struggled with her senses. Maria's face was blank. She was over in the far corner. She got up suddenly and crept closer to the others. Then the match burned his fingers. It went out.

He struck another. Four baleful eyes glared at him horridly: the mules. Castor and Pollux shuffled to his side. He felt them quiver. Even their fear was rhythmic; their hooves pattered. Besides the humans he now had two mules, two apes and a pair of reflex-jiggling donkeys watching him. They all smelled wet. The humans, too. The match scorched his fingers. And again it was velvety dark, darker than ordinary blackness, and there was no sound but the asthmatic sniffling of the mules.

'Is there a candle?' Maria whispered.

'No,' he said. There was. He didn't want to light it. He wasn't very scientific, but he knew that there was something in the air that was important both for breathing and burning. It was a big cavern. There was enough air to be breathed for quite some while. The candle didn't have to breathe, too. He thought humourlessly: you strike a match and if it doesn't burn you know the air is all used up. When that happens I will also know that I am dead.

He pointed himself at the entrance – where the entrance had been, rather – and went forward, hands out. He brushed Mother Beatrice familiarly and said, 'Excuse me,' and she said, 'It is all right.' He reached the wall of fallen stone that blocked it. He scrabbled at it. He tried to mount the slope. He couldn't get very high. It collapsed under him and ran in a dust-laden torrent down into the cavern. There was a mountainful of debris behind it. He shoved with his shoulder. Nothing yielded but his shirt. He tore it.

He heard Maria gasp. 'Well?'

'There's no hurry. At least we're out of the rain.'

'What sort of answer is that?'

He said coolly, 'Are you going to be a nuisance?'

'I will try not to be.' She breathed sharply in, then out.

'Good, my child,' Sister Ursula said happily. Caesar began to like her. He heard her stir over to Maria.

'You know what I'm going to do?' he said. 'I'm going back to sleep.'

'I don't think I could,' Maria said.

'Wait for the morning. We'll see what to do.'

'Nobody can see anything.'

'It's a figure of speech,' he said.

'How will you know it is morning?'

'I have a time-sense in my brain. It's as good as a clock.'

'You're a liar.'

'Yes. Now go to sleep.'

'You are sure it will be all right?'

'Sure.'

'It is really very cosy,' Sister Ursula said. 'Heaviness may endure for a night,' she quoted biblically, 'but joy cometh in the morning.'

'Who said that?'

It was a psalm. Sister Ursula knew them all. 'David,' she said.

'Was he ever in a cave?'

'Everybody, at some time in their life, is in a cave,' Sister Ursula said. 'Do you know, I am quite tired? There is nothing to fear.'

At her age, Caesar mused, what does she have to lose? He lay down. He propped his head in his hands. He listened to their breathing. Presently he heard Sister Ursula snore. He grinned. He wouldn't have expected a holy woman to snore. He couldn't hear Mother Beatrice. Nothing would make that grim woman sleep. Maria breathed lightly. Then sighed off. The mules occasionally coughed. There was a rustle in the cage and Caesar guessed that Number One was engaging Number Two in love. He grinned again. It wasn't very proper in the presence of nuns. He found it impossible to sleep. His brain was too active. He thought, this darkness is like a warm blanket: just pull it over your face and go to sleep. He couldn't. And he lay, staring into the pitchy darkness, wondering what to do, and whether life could end this easily – like snapping a rosebud off a twig.

I am no rosebud, he thought. I have a lot to do with my life. And the darkness weighed down on him. And the mules smelled. And Sister Ursula snored.

Major-General Brazzolo's detachment had been marching most of the afternoon. They were a motorized unit. Their leg muscles had become a little atrophied. They were more used to brake pedals. Now they were marching without pause into the dusk. The column had lost what little military smartness it possessed. They had broken up into trudging groups, some grumbling embitteredly, some too exhausted to speak. They knew everything there was to know: that they had a long way to go. That their boots were heavy. And that they had no rations.

A few had sticks of chocolate in their tunics, and these few kept this vital information to themselves. A stick of chocolate wouldn't feed a unit: but it would keep one man going. And now and again they chewed secretly, making the sweet saliva last a long time. Major-General Brazzolo marched at the head. His feet were swollen. He was a desk man. Sergeant Naso came behind. Lieutenant Arnolfo, that democratic officer, was half-way back along the column, mixed with the men.

He found himself trudging behind the Pirellis. Their endurance amazed him. Luigi, with the tub belly, marched as if his life depended on it – as, in fact, it did. He sweated. He didn't speak with his mouth. He husbanded his breath. But his hands kept up a running conversation with his wife, who understood every anguished word they said. Her twitching eyes were glazed. But she walked upright, turning now and again to glare defiantly at the men.

Sophia, the daughter, simply walked. She was a strong girl. She wanted to live. She was hungry. She knew that there would be food at the end of the journey. And so she simply walked.

'One, two, three,' Sergeant Naso called back mechanically, trying to keep the detachment in step. Nobody took much notice of him. He didn't expect them to. It was merely a barrack-yard habit.

He fell back to join Lieutenant Arnolfo. 'Do you know how far we have to go?' he asked.

'Yes.'

'Do you think we shall make it?'

'Do we have any alternative?'

'My stomach is growling. I am starving.'

Lieutenant Arnolfo remembered some of the things the sergeant used to bark at the troops. He quoted them bitterly, 'A soldier is discipline on two legs, he is an example of fortitude to his comrades, he suppresses all appetites in the face of duty . . .'

'All right. That's enough,' Sergeant Naso said.

'There are some men eating chocolate. How about one of us pulling rank?'

'It wouldn't be fair. I have a stick, too.'

'Be an example to a comrade.'

'Here.' The sergeant gave him half the stick. 'If ever we get back,' which he doubted, 'I shall ask to be transferred to the field,' he said. 'These technical units are too dangerous.' He went forward to rejoin the major-general.

The major-general felt enormously lonely. He would be blamed for everything, of course. That was the burden of command. He couldn't remember having made a single error of judgment. And from the moment he'd entered the stricken village of Lorenzo of the Angels – curiously connected with that fair-haired unItalian boy – nothing had gone right. He wondered bitterly what had happened to the boy. He should suffer a little, too. His feelings would have been very mixed if he'd known what was about to happen to him.

He glanced at the men and said exasperatedly to the sergeant, 'Tell them to be cheerful.'

Did he expect them to sing?

'Yes, major-general,' the sergeant said.

'We shall survive. You have my personal promise. We shall be in Naples in two days.'

The sergeant looked at him woodenly. There is no real

Italian equivalent for the cynicism: in a pig's ear. But it was exactly how he felt.

Lieutenant Arnolfo simply put one foot in line with the other and kept going. There was an iron band about his pelvis as if he were in imminent danger of giving birth. His calves ached. He straightened up. He wanted to be what Sergeant Naso had unashamedly called an 'example of fortitude' to his men. Whereas the sergeant didn't believe a word of it, Lieutenant Arnolfo did. He tried to take the army seriously. He wasn't suited to it. What soldiers most need, as Sergeant Naso could have told him, is a certain coarseness of fibre, and Lieutenant Arnolfo was much too sensitive a man. He read far too much, which is bad for officers, for it puts seeds of doubt in their minds.

Officers must never doubt. It confuses their readiness to obey orders. It makes them suspect their commanders.

And Lieutenant Arnolfo stared hard at Major-General Brazzolo and suspected him.

They were in a bad way. They had suffered disaster after disaster. Major-generals were supposed to be there to see that they didn't happen. They would always happen to Major-General Brazzolo. He was the wrong shape for a commander. The lieutenant watched him wryly and thought: we have no Caesar there. Thinking of Caesar brought the boy and his marble head back to his mind. Suddenly, in a flash of bitter understanding, he knew that the boy was at the root of all their troubles. He had goaded the major-general into an emotional state in which he wasn't capable of making a right decision. I would like to throw him over that cliff, he thought.

Then he grinned. No, I wouldn't. *There* is a budding Caesar. That ancient head has got into the right hands. And at that moment he saw the Pirelli daughter, Sophia, looking at him sidelong, and because he was sorry for her, as he would have been sorry for any female in distress, even one as revoltingly ugly as this, he smiled pleasantly back.

It was foolish of him. He could make wrong decisions, too. She was a peasant with lumpish instincts. Men usually didn't look at her. Much less smile. She misinterpreted it. Her heart gave a throb. She thought: how handsome he is. He nodded to her as if to say: thumbs up. Everything will be all right. It encouraged her to do something mad. No girl with a father like Luigi of the talking hands and a mother with the twitching eye of a gorgon could be anything but a little mad.

She dropped back until she was level with him. She gave him another stealthy sexual look. She giggled to herself. She pretended to droop with exhaustion. He was startled to feel her fall slantwise right into his arms.

He had to grab her, and in doing so he enfolded her ample breasts. The men behind stared. Nobody helped. The mother looked round and saw him recoil from the grab at her breasts. She shouted, 'What are you doing to her?'

'She fell . . .'

'Let her be. Animal. Cannot you do without a woman? She is an innocent child.'

'Ask anybody. She is worn out . . .'

'Sophia,' Luigi cried.

She giggled at him faintly.

'There is no relief from these beasts. There is only one thing they want. Even in public. Signor Major-general,' the mother yelled, and he came back. 'Cannot you control your men?'

'What happened?'

'Assault. A physical assault on the child's modesty. I saw it with my own eyes,' Luigi said: and his jabbing fingers pictured rape and feminine despair.

The major-general stared at her incredulously.

'She collapsed,' Lieutenant Arnolfo said.

'Why are you holding her there?'

The lieutenant released himself from her bosom and shoved her aside.

Luigi came very close. 'Is a helpless girl to be mauled?' The major-general recoiled from his garlic as the lieutenant had recoiled from Sophia's breasts.

'Keep your fingers out of my eyes.'

'Is she to be denied protection?'

'Wolves. We are in the midst of wolves,' Luigi's wife howled. 'Wolves with unashamed lusts.' The men fell back from her. They didn't look like wolves. They were afraid of her glittering eye.

'Get ahead,' the major-general muttered to the lieutenant. He flurried him on.

When they got to the head of the column he said angrily, 'What sort of stupid thing was that?'

'What are you suggesting?'

'She is ugly. How could you want to touch her?'

'She collapsed.'

'That was a funny way to collapse. You were holding her ——' using the colloquial Italian for tits.

'On my honour. I swear it. It never occurred to me . . .'

'Wait till we get to Naples. There'll be time enough for it,' the major-general said. He had to talk to somebody. 'We are in trouble.'

The lieutenant was still sweating from his trouble. He looked up. The sky was hazing over ominously. Rain, too. To add to their trouble. He shrank from the first stinging drop.

'I do not think we are going to make it,' the major-general said.

The lieutenant gave him a strange look. He couldn't believe his ears.

'What do you mean?'

'Do you know how far we have to go?'

'I heard you tell the sergeant we would be in Naples in two days . . .'

'Do you think I am mad? We don't want the men to know. It will take four days. We will have to march all night. Without food. What do you think we eat in this wilderness? Grass? By tomorrow they will be dropping in the ditches.'

The hard spatter thickened. The drops smacked like spent bullets in the dust. The lieutenant shivered. He stared up at the peaks. They vanished in a thick swirl of grey-black cloud. It was much worse up there. Somewhere along one of those distant ledges, at that moment, Caesar was harrying the anguished mules through a deluge.

The lieutenant found his voice. 'What are you going to do?'

'Leave them where they drop. As far as I am concerned that Pirelli family can be the first to go,' the major-general said.

For a moment the lieutenant thought it was an act of staggering ruthlessness. Then he stared at the plump haunted face and knew that it was an act of weakness. And *this* is a commander, he raged. That boy – that nothing, that undersized Caesar in knee-pants – is more of a leader. He said violently, 'I will never agree.'

'You will do as you are told.'

'We cannot abandon them . . .'

'Better for some of us to get through than none at all.'

Then it came down in a sheet. The lieutenant didn't bother to turn up his collar. Before he could gasp he was drenched. He ran back.

Sergeant Naso caught his arm as he passed. 'What did he say?'

'Nothing.'

'Listen,' the sergeant said grimly, forgetting rank. 'I am

a senior non-com. I have been in the army longer than you. You can tell me.'

'He doesn't think we are going to make it.'

'I will,' the sergeant said. 'If I have to crawl on my hands and knees. I have a wife and children.'

'Without food?'

'So I will chew my knuckles.' The sergeant stared venomously at the sodden round figure of the major-general. 'He doesn't have to worry, does he? He can live off his fat like a camel.'

The lieutenant ran on. He passed Sophia. She had her coat over her head. She opened the folds to ogle him. He pretended not to see. He rejoined the men for whom he felt a great pity. And the rain lashed along the valley and they were all too miserable to talk and the dragging boots went: squelch, squelch, squelch.

It was warm in the cave. The air was growing thick. There was no sound but the slurry breath of the sleeping donkeys. The mules reeked. Caesar could almost point himself at them like a radar beacon. He listened to Sister Ursula's old throat. She whistled in her sleep. And there was no sight at all. He tried to pierce the almost-to-be-felt darkness and thought: it must be like this in the grave. He started to get up. He had forgotten that he was still holding Number Two's hand. She whimpered drowsily. He patted her. 'Not going far,' he whispered through the bars. There really wasn't anywhere he could go.

He felt his way round to the rear cage. He went on groping by touch until he fondled the marble head under the straw. What would you do? he wondered.

He fingered the imperious lips. They didn't move. He found himself echoing the thoughts in that two-thousand-year-old brain. Muster your strength, it said. Harden your will. The greatest victories are won when all seems lost.

What is the joy of an easy triumph? I conquered the world by the power and passion of my will.

But there is nothing to fight. Just a blocked cave. What do I use my will on?

On yourself, the stone head said. Your mind is your weapon. Sharpen it. Conquer this cave.

Yes. How?

How did I take Gaul? It was there to be taken. I took it.

H'mm, Caesar mused. It seemed a sterile sort of sermon. He let go of the marble and groped on up. He felt the folds of the virgin's cloak. He reached up until he was fondling the child's face. He hoped God wouldn't mind the familiarity. He didn't want to rouse the others. He lowered his voice to the barest whisper. 'Listen, God. Did I wake you? I'm sorry. How about this business? It's a bit of a problem for you, too.'

He went on stroking the child's face in the blackness, feeling perhaps for a movement of the lips.

'Let's face it,' he murmured. 'You're not going to be much of a God buried in the dark. You can't run a whole world by remote control. You have to be there. You run the sunshine. You have to see it. You have to watch people. They are all going to forget you if you stay locked up in here.'

He felt for the virgin's face. It was still wet with rain. A drop ran down his finger. It was rather like a tear.

'Talk to God. You're his mother. He has to listen. Ask him what about it. Could he work maybe a small miracle?'

He waited politely. Sister Ursula's throat went on whistling.

'Nothing very special,' he said. 'Nothing like healing lepers. Say, like a little landslide. Just a shove with his shoulders and he could get rid of that rock.'

The tears on the virgin's face went on running down his wrist. 'No need to cry. I'm just trying to be practical. See what you can do about it. Talk to him. I'll be here.' And Caesar chuckled humourlessly: there wasn't anywhere else he could be.

He heard a quick breath very close to him and smelled the slight mustiness of Mother Beatrice's damp robe. She was so close that he could almost feel her heat. He wondered how long she'd been eavesdropping. He felt angry.

'You believe,' she said in a trembling voice. 'I knew it. You ask for help. It will come. We all seek him in tribulation.' Her voice rose triumphantly. He thought she was mad. 'This is your act of faith.'

'Do you always listen to private conversations?'

'We all share one conversation. Our heart's yearning for God.'

'I'm just yearning to get out. So far he hasn't been much help.'

'But you believe.'

It was a little silly. He shrugged away.

'Seek him while he is near,' she said.

Caesar didn't see how he could be much nearer. He could actually reach up and touch his face.

'You'll wake the others.'

'I am awake,' Sister Ursula said. He heard Maria cough. They were all up. He heard the rustle of straw in the other cage where Numbers One and Two stirred. He felt the hard shove of a furry rump against him. It was Pollux. The mules sounded off intestinally in their corner. Noah, surrounded by the animal kingdom, must have felt the same kind of claustrophobia in the ark. Only the ark was never as dark as this.

'Come closer,' Sister Ursula said. 'We cannot see each other. But we can at least feel each other's comfort.' The donkeys' harness jingled. The mules sniffled. 'Yes, the animals, too. They also need comfort. I am going to tell you a story,' she said.

Caesar sighed. He guessed where it was going to come from. There are a lot of good stories in it. But I can't think of one that will get us out of here, he thought.

'There was once a man of Gaza,' Sister Ursula said. 'He had had the strength of ten. And now he was weak. He was a prisoner in the house of his persecutors. For him, too, all was dark.' Samson, Caesar recollected. He had heard of him. He pricked up his ears. He was always interested in strong men. 'And in this hour of his deepest darkness he called out in despair to the Lord.'

Sister Ursula's frail voice drifted staunchly across the cave. She is a good story-teller, Caesar thought. She is good for children. He wondered if the donkeys were listening. They were very still.

'Hope had almost gone,' she said. 'These are the times when men are truly tried. When hope has gone with the light, and faith is trapped in the dark. For this man the darkness was utter: for his enemies had put out his eyes.'

'Samson,' Maria announced. Caesar hushed her impatiently. She was a little slow in catching on.

'And this man, in his blindness,' Sister Ursula said, 'begged the lad who led him to let him feel the pillars of the house. Let me lean upon them, he said.'

Caesar felt Mother Beatrice's hand suddenly grip his. She was still trembling. He couldn't think what had got into her.

'And Samson lifted up his head and said, Lord, remember me, I pray thee, this last time give me strength.' Sister Ursula was now quoting pretty directly from the book. Her memory was perfect. 'And he took hold of the two pillars, one with his right hand, the other with his left, and he bowed himself with all his might. And the house of his persecutors fell.'

Caesar heard Maria sigh. He didn't see the connection.

Did they expect him to take hold of the rubble that sealed the cave and bow with all his might?

It wouldn't fall. He'd tried it. All he'd got was a torn sleeve.

'He *believed*,' Mother Beatrice said. She was hurting his wrist. He released himself. She said passionately, 'It was an act of faith.'

He didn't like women to be too passionate. Passion belonged to men.

'It doesn't move rock.'

'It moves mountains,' she said.

She was out of this world. Numbers One and Two had suddenly started to whimper. He wondered what was the matter with them.

'I feel sorry for you,' Maria said. 'You don't believe in anything.'

Only in me, he thought. He said, 'Be quiet,' to the apes. They went on whimpering. They rattled the bars of the cage.

He struck a match. At the instant of the first glitter, before the flame made their eyes swivel, he saw them looking up. He looked up, too.

He let the match go out. He accustomed his eyes to the dark. He saw the pale glitter of a star. He moved his head. It vanished. He moved again and it came back.

'There is a hole up there,' he said.

'Where?' Sister Ursula said calmly. He thought for a moment of sheer disbelief that she almost expected it.

He fumbled for his stub of a candle. He lit it. He'd lost the direction of the hole, but the apes could still sense it. Or smell it. They were staring up.

He released them from the cage. They seemed a little startled by the sudden freedom. They looked at him pathetically. Their eyes said: no chains?

He was taking no chances. He roped them by the neck,

leaving the rope in a wide loop between them. He took hold
of the middle of it. 'Go on,' he said to them softly. 'Show
us.'

They went in a quick scamper up the rubble. The rope
tugged. He saw Number Two vanish for an instant. She
was through the hole.

'Not so fast,' and he tugged her back. 'Wait for me.' He
went up the rope after them, using them as an anchor. They
struggled under his weight. They held. He came up to them
and felt a quick breath of cool air. He looked out through
the gap at the stars. The rain had stopped. There was a big
moon.

He half edged his body through. Numbers One and Two
were already out. And then he had the sickening sensation
that it was all yielding beneath him: the piled rubble,
jammed precariously, began to slip and rumble, and he was
going with it – head over heels, caught in a great stony
cascade, pebbles tearing his hands. He was in terrible pain
from the hammering as he rolled down, beaten and grazed,
and he thought the bone of his cheek was broken when he
finally stopped rolling. He was half buried.

He felt his face. He looked at the smear on his hand.
Blood was black in the moon.

The apes had torn loose. They sat trembling, roped together, half-way up the cliff.

He heard Maria calling in the cave, now blocked only by
the low collapsed mound. He didn't know why she didn't
come out. Then he saw Mother Beatrice scramble over it
delicately. Sister Ursula came next: then Maria. He went
back and started dragging the mound down. When it was
knee-high he hitched the mules to the front cage. One at a
time. 'Pull,' he said. They stared at him reluctantly. 'Pull,'
he ordered. 'Or you know what I will do to you.' They
knew. They never forgot their tender rumps.

They dragged the cage over what was left of the rubble.

It bounced and it banged. He thought the bent wheel would never survive it. He took the mules back for the second cage and rescued that, too. God and his mother lurched in it. They took a stiff jolting. He saw Mother Beatrice watching with her heart in her mouth. Then he went back for the donkeys, waiting patiently. He patted them. Only they have dignity, he thought.

'Are you hurt?' This was Sister Ursula.

'I'm hurt all over. It doesn't matter. I don't crack.'

Maria began to shiver. She should be grateful for life: and all she does is shiver. He looked at her with contempt.

He called up to Numbers One and Two, 'Come on back.'

They crouched, half-way up the cliff, shivering, too. He knew suddenly that they weren't going to come back. They stared yearningly into his eyes. He stared into theirs. They'd tasted freedom: and it was very sweet. He tried to reach the dangling rope. They scampered a little higher and dragged it beyond his hands.

He sighed. He felt very sad. 'All right,' he said. 'You deserve it. Go on. You are free.'

They understood him. They looked fleetingly at Maria. She was crying. Then, in a quick grey whisk, they were gone. Caesar wanted to cry, too. He wondered how they would exist in these cold hills in the winter.

I have lost three good friends, he thought. First Lucrezia. Now these. I have never had many friends. If this goes on I shall soon have no friends at all.

Mother Beatrice repeated tranquilly, 'Faith moves mountains.'

Caesar gave her an angry look.

'Thank God for his miracle,' she said.

He bridled. 'What did he have to do with it? It was the apes who found the hole.'

'He directed them.'

'He has cost me my friends.'

'He will guard them.'

'They will freeze to death.' It had been an expensive miracle. He was still very upset. It was getting near to dawn. There was a pallor in a corner of the sky. He knew that Mother Beatrice and Sister Ursula wanted to rest. He didn't intend to let them. He looked coldly at God and his mother and thought: nor you, too. He climbed on the cage and said to Maria, 'Get up.' She was still crying. Tears annoyed him. He took it out on the mules with a quick hard kick. They were the most aggrieved of all. They dragged at the cages and the skewed wheel went: hup, hup, hup.

XII

How quiet it is, Caesar thought. He waited for a bird to sing. It was as if the terrible violation of the forest had scared them off. Perhaps when the dawn came they would begin. He blew on his hands. It was very cold. The valley was choked with mist. Nothing poked out of it but the tops of the tallest trees. It muffled every sound: the squeak of the cages, the clop of the mules, the frisky patter of the donkeys' hooves. They were alive and grateful. They showed it by doing little *entrechats* like ballerinas. It was also to keep them warm.

They went snaking down into the valley – the mules no longer needed to drag. The cages pressed on their rumps. They grumbled out of habit. Nothing satisfied them.

I am hungry again, Caesar thought. Maria watched him poignantly as if to say: I am hollow. He grinned. So am I. Hit my belly and it will ring like a bell. He glanced at Mother Beatrice and Sister Ursula. They are used to fasting. Religion is a good training for a journey like this. They had chosen to sit together at the back. They looked pale and worn. Their robes were ragged. They don't like me any more, he thought. They've given me up. They've stopped trying to possess me.

He was wrong. Far from not liking him, they were entranced with him. They would never give him up – they were more than ever determined to possess him. His immortal soul at least. The very spirit and essence of him. It came to the same thing.

Mother Beatrice was sixty-five. Sister Ursula was sixty.

He had ignited a sense of purpose and passion in them. It was their last spiritual fling. The moment he turned away they watched him jealously. They were proud of him.

Sister Ursula whispered, 'You know who he reminds me of? The child Eli, chosen of the Lord.'

Mother Beatrice thought this was a little extreme. It was taking biblical licence. Saul, perhaps. Saul the warrior-king. 'Hush,' she said fondly.

'He has great power. He will be a blessing. He is destined for remarkable things.'

'There is no need to let him hear. It will only turn his head.'

'He will be a blessing to us, too.'

'Yes, yes. Now hush,' Mother Beatrice said.

Caesar heard them muttering. They are talking about me, he thought. It can't be very good. It's just too bad. One can't be both good and strong.

They were descending faster and faster. The forest thickened. Up in the mountains the devastation had been awesome. Here it was ludicrous: the trees tumbled like clowns. It wasn't unusual to see great earthy roots thrust up into the sky where the branches should have been. There should have been hamlets, too. There were the caved-in roofs of farmhouses, stones piled like cairns. The scavenging birds were busy in the gloaming. And suddenly the dawn flashed.

The first ray pricked Caesar like a hot needle. The mist in the valley grew pink. If Caesar had been able to pierce it – if he had been able to look over the screen of the trees – he would have seen Major-General Brazzolo's detachment rise like exhausted ghosts from the ditch and continue their march.

They had rested an hour. It was too cold to sleep. They huddled together for warmth, discussing hunger. And hatred of bureaucracy. Hatred of the army. Including Sergeant

Naso, who drove them cruelly. And Major-General Brazzolo most of all.

They said: soldiers need a leader. That is why we have major-generals. To lead us. This man is a scientist. He knows all about wave-bands and oscilloscopes, but he does not know how to lead. Look at him. He is too fat. They insulted him in every breath. The army had no right to let him out of his office. He has landed us in this mess.

Lieutenant Arnolfo thought: he just cannot give men hope. He is no Napoleon. He cannot screw them to the last desperate pitch of effort. Come to that, neither can I.

Luigi Pirelli lay silent. His fingers talked on their own. They said: you are hungry. He knew it. You are lost. He knew that, too. You will not live to see another dawn. He moaned. His wife, who was better material than he was, glared. Her unfortunate eye twitched.

Sergeant Naso thought grimly: I am going to get back if I have to leave them all lying in a ditch. It isn't the proper army spirit. But I have a wife and children. To hell with the army spirit. I will walk while I have legs.

Major-General Brazzolo knew that he had lost his men's confidence. He didn't know what to do about it. Something was beginning to obsess him. I wish I had driven straight through the village of Lorenzo of the Angels, he thought. I didn't see any angels. All I saw was that boy. Everything began with him. He is my bad-luck piece. I hope he is also lying cold and forlorn in a ditch.

Hardly ten kilometres off Caesar was sitting, cold but not forlorn, on the cage. Food will turn up somewhere, he thought. We have God with us. Let him earn his keep.

And suddenly they came on the village. They turned a bend and saw ruins. A woman sitting like a heap of discarded rags on a collapsed wall saw them and shouted. Men came out of the hovels. There were gaunt. hollow-eyed children. They looked like spectres. 'Stop,' Mother Beatrice said.

And Caesar stopped, not because she had told him to, but because the men had formed a quick phalanx across the road to bar their way.

Do nothing, Caesar thought. Say nothing. Let them say something. He waited courteously for somebody to speak. Nobody spoke. They watched him. And because the silence was a kind of stalemate, and it was beginning to annoy him, he watched them.

He stared about the village. This place has been shaved, he thought. A razor has been across it. The church was a stump. Nobody had shifted the debris. The hovels had been nothing to begin with. Now they were heaps of wattle and plaster. He counted ten grown men and six women. He didn't count the gaunt children.

He looked at their blown bellies and thought: they have crawled like worms out of the ground.

What are these people? Primitives? What has happened to their tongues? They just watched him with a flat-eyed intensity. He felt a little like the trail-leader of a wagon-train that had rolled into an Indian village that had never seen a white man before.

The mules were restless. They jerked. The cages rolled forward a metre or two. The men moved closer: made a more solid bar across the road.

It was very significant. Caesar, for no reason he cared to analyse, felt his skin crawl.

They are all touched. It was altogether too quiet. At sun-up chickens squawked in a village. Cows lowed. Nothing squawked and nothing lowed. Caesar knew why. They have eaten everything that survived ruin and fire. He looked at their slightly-mad faces and thought: what do they do next? Eat us?

Maria asked curiously – she wasn't in the least frightened – 'What is the matter with them?'

'They are hungry.' Caesar wasn't particularly frightened, either. Simply on edge.

'We are hungry, too.'

There were degrees of hunger. He looked at the villagers again and thought: they are nothing but bones with eyes.

A woman held a child to her breast. Caesar had no sexual feelings about women's breasts. He stared at it. It was dry. The child started a thin wail that died off like a squeezed bagpipe. It was too weak to cry.

We had better get out of here. Caesar touched the reins, and the mules heaved, and the woman with the child laid it shockingly in front of their hooves. They stopped. Mother Beatrice froze. Caesar heard Sister Ursula give a broken whisper. They are never much help, are they?

He sighed. He picked out three people he expected to give him most trouble. There was a thick-shouldered man with a bleak face. There was the dry-breasted woman with the child. There was an old grandmother with wild, infuriated eyes. 'Is something wrong?' he asked.

'Yes,' the man with the bleak face said. 'Something is wrong. We starve.'

'We have all had trouble.'

'We can see our trouble. We cannot see yours.'

Everybody sees his own trouble. 'We have a long way to go,' Caesar said. 'And nothing to eat.'

'We have nowhere to go,' the man told him. 'And we also have nothing to eat.'

It was talking in circles. Caesar thought: I am sorry for them. But there is nothing I can do. I cannot stay here all day swapping misery. He made to touch the reins, expecting the woman with the child to pick it up. She let it lie. The grandmother with the frantic eyes breathed in and out like a bellows. She was as bent as a hook. Caesar wondered how she stood. She wasn't looking at him. She was looking at the mules. She reminded him of a toothless animal that might manage one more bite. 'If we had food we would share it with you,' Caesar said.

'You have food,' the man with the bleak face said.

'We have nothing.'

'You have food,' the man repeated.

'I have just told you no ——' and Caesar's blood chilled. It was an extraordinary sensation. The grandmother was feeling the mules.

It was the prod of a careful housewife at the butcher's. Maria watched her without understanding. Sister Ursula, too. But Mother Beatrice's mouth was a tight bloodless line. She understood.

The woman picked up the child. She stuffed her nipple uselessly in its mouth. The grandmother was now pinching the donkeys. Caesar flinched. The crone took hold of a lump of Pollux's fur to feel the flesh of the rump. She looked at Caesar. This is an old cannibal, he thought. I will kill her. He was shaking with rage. I had better do something. 'We will be on our way,' he said.

'Yes. But get down first,' the bleak-faced man said. 'And leave the donkeys and the mules.'

'We have too far to go.'

'We have to eat. You and the women can walk.'

'To Rome?'

The woman with the child said emptily. 'To hell, if you wish. My child has to eat.'

Now even Maria understood. She wailed.

Caesar watched the men stretch in a line across the road. He counted them. Three of them were ancients. They didn't worry him. The others weren't too formidable, either. Chiefly it was the man with the bleak face. It was rather a sad face. I am sad for you, too, Caesar thought. But you are not going to eat our mules. Much less Castor and Pollux. That would be like eating one's friends.

Then he was surprised to find that his blood was racing.

It pleased him enormously. He wasn't frightened at all. He said to Maria, 'Be quiet.' The tears were running down her face. 'They're nobody's dinner yet.' He got down from the cage.

They looked at him. He wore knee-pants. He didn't look too formidable, either. He walked round to the back cage. He fumbled under the straw. He heard the jingle of harness as one of the men began to unstrap the mules. They didn't protest. They'll protest loud enough when they feel the knife, he thought. We need them. There isn't going to be any knife. He felt the cold touch of the marble and caught a glimpse of the *imperator*'s head. 'It's all right,' he said to it softly. 'Don't worry. You won't be ashamed of me.' He felt for the shotgun. It didn't work. Only he knew it. He caught sight of the virgin: and he gave the child at her knee a quick cynical glance. 'You don't do much when you're needed, do you? Isn't it about time you began to earn your keep?' And then he went round with the shotgun: cocked it: let the men see that his fingers didn't shake.

And he pointed it at the belly of the man with the bleak face.

'I will kill you if I have to,' he said. 'Get out of our way.'

The man looked at the shotgun. 'No, you won't,' he said.

'Try me.'

'How many could you kill?'

'Two to begin with.'

'We will die, anyway, if we starve.' The man shrugged indifferently. 'What difference does it make?'

'Nobody gives up hope,' Caesar said.

'Hope,' the woman with the child screamed. 'Here.' She made to thrust it at Caesar. He recoiled from it. 'Here is my hope. It is dying,' she said.

Then Caesar heard Mother Beatrice's voice from the top of the cage. He was staggered. 'In the name of Christ,' she said faintly. 'Give them the mules.'

'Are you mad?'

'Let us all be a little mad. For charity's sake.' She got down. 'They are starving. Let them have the beasts.'

'And walk?'

'We have legs. They will carry us.'

'You are an old woman.'

She almost laughed. It cracked like a nut in her throat. 'We will surprise you.' She beckoned to Sister Ursula. She got down, too. He looked angrily at the two ragged nuns: they keep blunting me all the time, he thought. They just won't let a man's blade stay sharp. He stared at the child. The wet peaked face disgusted him. The mother buried its dribble in her breast. He made a hopeless gesture and threw the shotgun into the ditch.

They might have dared him, anyway. They'd have discovered that it didn't work.

He saw the grandmother untying the donkeys. He grabbed hold of her shoulder and whirled her round. She was so bent that her face was almost level with his. 'Leave them alone,' he cried.

She grinned. She had two astoundingly blackened teeth. He wondered how they could have got into a human mouth. 'They will cook better than the mules,' she said.

'Don't touch them.' He was shaking. He didn't know what to say. He said the first words that came to his lips. 'They are holy. They are God's donkeys.'

She peered at him. She is the ugliest old woman I have ever seen, he thought.

'Look behind you. Go on. We have God in that cage,' he said.

The bleak-faced man said cynically, 'We used to have him in the church.' He looked at the broken stump. He seemed to be angry about it. He started to drag Castor off. Pollux followed automatically. Where one went the other went. 'Well, he isn't there any more,' he said.

Caesar wetted his lips. If I'd had a shotgun that worked it might have been better to shoot him, he thought.

'I just told you. He's in the cage.'

'Wherever he is.' Castor pulled loose. The two donkeys nuzzled up to Caesar. The man grabbed at the ropes. He seemed to be getting angry with Caesar, too.

'See for yourself,' Caesar said.

The old crone went round. She stared into the cage. She touched the virgin. The straw rustled. It was rank. It doesn't smell very holy, Caesar thought. The woman with the child followed. Caesar held his breath. There was a dragging silence. The old men were trying to absorb the idea. They watched him uneasily. Then, out of the corner of his eye, Caesar saw the old grandmother cross herself, and he shivered. The knot in his stomach loosened. They are all as superstitious as crows, he thought.

He felt the soft shove of the donkeys' rumps and thought: if I play this carefully you will not end up as anybody's dinner.

'We have to take God to Rome. These are his personal donkeys,' he said.

'You talk too much,' the man said.

'They are very special. Watch,' Caesar said.

He beckoned to Maria. 'Show them,' he said. She wasn't listening. She was white-faced. The tears gushed from her eyes. He snapped his fingers and she stared at him. She woke up.

'Sing,' he said.

She began to sing in a choked unaffected voice. It was a happy song – Verdi's 'Di quell' amor ch'e palpito' in which, as the lyric suggests, Violetta palpitates with love – and the tears ran miserably down her face. The donkeys strutted. The ears flashed up. They went instantly into the dance. Caesar heard the grandmother hiss. The woman with the child turned its wet dazed face so that it could watch.

Castor did an *arabesque*: knees dipped, fairy fashion, rump up. Pollux matched it with an elegant *glissade*: a sideways lilt as in a skater's waltz. The hooves twinkled. Now they went into a joint *pas de bourrée*: nothing is quite so difficult as this. Particularly for donkeys. They achieved it with grace.

Even the bleak-faced man was moved. His eyes grew just that little less bleak. Watching him, Caesar thought with a triumphant swell: Big Julius should be proud. The old crone's mouth sagged. He looked away from the blackened teeth.

'*Di quell' amor*,' Maria sang, and the donkeys twirled in a last pirouette. Caesar snapped his fingers. It was enough.

'You cannot eat donkeys like these,' he said. 'They are God's miracles. He needs them to get him to Rome.'

The old men watched him. He saw empty bellies struggling with awe. He thought: they are nothing but primitives. It was worth taking a risk. He said, 'Do you have to anger God? Lay a hand on them and you know what will happen? Haven't you read the bible? Plagues.' He raised his voice suddenly and acted a couple of them out. 'Boils,' he said, clapping his hands to his neck. 'Locusts in millions to eat up your crops.' He made a crawling motion to picture locusts eating up the crops. It was overdoing it, of course. 'Then darkness. Unending darkness,' putting his hand over his eyes. Sister Ursula looked confused. He saw Mother Beatrice watching him with shock.

I'm just giving them a little of her religious medicine, he thought. It wasn't quite the same thing. She thought angrily: he is misusing it. I still think it was a creditable performance, he thought.

'You have a terrible tongue,' the man said.

'Keep the mules. But leave us the donkeys.'

'Take them. Go on. Before we change our minds.'

Caesar's stomach stretched. He didn't want the man to hear his gasp of relief.

He hitched the donkeys to God's cage. They looked diminutive between the shafts. One cage was as much as they could haul; he left the other by the roadside. At least we are shut of that skewed wheel, he thought. He said peremptorily to Maria, 'Get down.' There would be no more riding. He looked grimly at the two nuns, thinking: now let's see you use your legs. He put his bundle in with God. He murmured to the donkeys, 'Try. You carry an important passenger.' They were so tiny. But their eyes shone. He patted their rumps. They were wet with sweat. You just danced for your lives, he thought.

'Pull,' he said. They pulled. The cage creaked off. He hitched up his belt and walked alongside with Maria and the nuns.

'Boy,' the bleak-faced man called out. 'Wait.'

Caesar's heart sank.

'Take a little of the mules to eat on the way.'

Caesar stared at them. He hadn't loved them very much. They had wicked tempers: they'd never ceased to smell. But they'd brought them a long way. 'It's all right,' he said. He'd lost his appetite. He looked at Maria. Her eyes glittered with sentimental tears. 'Keep it. You need it more than we do.' He was paraphrasing Sir Philip Sidney of whom he'd never heard.

They trudged through the line of villagers. The old crone ran a few steps after the cage to kiss the virgin. Then the stump of the church and the ruined hovels were behind and it was the lost, lonely, open road all the way.

Mother Beatrice's face was dark. Caesar looked at her. 'Is something wrong?' he asked.

'Yes.' She was angry. 'The things you told those people. You were not sincere.'

'How do you know?'

'You didn't mean a word you said.'

'Some words no,' he admitted. 'Some words yes. Does it matter?'

'Yes,' she flashed. 'Truth matters.'

Caesar was astonished to hear Sister Ursula burst out, 'Gratitude matters, too.'

Mother Beatrice was as astonished as Caesar. For perhaps ten seconds she was lost for words.

'We have forgotten to thank him,' Sister Ursula said. She was very pale. She was trembling. 'We are not practical women. We are a burden he carries on his back.'

Now that's talking, Caesar thought.

Sister Ursula stared defiantly at her Mother-Superior. She had never spoken to her this way. 'He has fed us. He has encouraged us. We do not know what we owe him. We are still moving. At least God is on his way.'

Caesar chuckled to himself. He would never have thought this dedicated little shell of a woman had it in her.

'I am sorry,' Sister Ursula said. 'But *that* is the truth that matters. It had to be said.' And because she was still pale and trembling she tossed her head and walked on by herself.

They were walking in a straight line – without knowing it – towards a meeting with Major-General Brazzolo's men. They were somewhere down there. Caesar couldn't see them. Before it had been the cold morning fog. Now it was the afternoon heat-haze. The soldiers were dragging along, looking like the skeletal remnant of some lost exploratory band. The sun was at its zenith. It dried them up. The dust rose, coating their faces, filling their mouths. They had almost run out of saliva: they couldn't spit themselves free of it.

There was a shocking silence in the column, broken only by the crunch of their boots. They were too exhausted to talk. When eloquent Italians can no longer talk they are very near the base of despair.

Some of them had thrown away their tunics because of the heat. This was foolish. It was very cold at night. They were learning another bitter lesson: not to take boots off swollen feet. It was hard to get them on again. Their stomachs burped emptily. Some of them chewed grass, which made them vomit. They were strung out in little local groups, men from the same Sicilian village joining up. There was no pretence of military formation.

It made Lieutenant Arnolfo, looking back, think of the disastrous retreat from Moscow. This was a disaster, too, but it was a retreat from an earthquake in the lost Abruzzi.

Sergeant Naso looked back, too. The formation would normally have sickened him. He knew that if he didn't eat by nightfall he would be even sicker. He was hollow. He looked at Major-General Brazzolo, six paces ahead, and thought: there is a fine fat rump. It would fry very well.

The major-general was drenched with sweat. He carried a lot of weight. He had untied his laces to let his feet bulge. They were agonizing. He would have died rather than show it. He knew that he might still die.

He was still sure that he wasn't to blame. The sun made his head ache. It gave him fanciful ideas. He thought unjustly, that boy is laughing somewhere. In hell, I hope. I will soon join him.

He heard a cry. He turned. Luigi Pirelli had dropped into the ditch. He lay as if dead. His wife was shaking him. She was a Tuscan, and almost indestructible. She was prepared to walk until the soles were worn off her feet. The daughter, Sophia, now fell into the ditch. The men dragged to a stop. They watched them pitilessly.

The major-general felt sick with exasperation. He went back. 'Get them to their feet,' he said.

146

Lieutenant Arnolfo was trying to drag Luigi up. 'I can't.'

'Time is running out. Doesn't he understand? We have to push on.'

'He says he is finished.'

'He will be if he stays here.'

Sophia pressed her face into the earth and wept.

'Get up,' the major-general said thickly. He could hardly stand himself.

Luigi's fingers, which seemed to be the only live parts of him, said: my legs are dead. Leave me here.

The major-general sighed. The men watched him with contempt. He heard the dragging scuffle of their boots. They had resumed their march.

He said angrily over his shoulder, 'Halt.'

They passed him in scattered lethargic groups. They looked at him as if he were a stranger.

'Did you hear me? Halt,' the major-general cried.

They ignored him. He watched the tail-end of the column drift down the road. Something as cold and sharp as an icicle formed in his heart. He had lost control of his men.

He gave Lieutenant Arnolfo a ghastly look. 'Stop them,' he said.

The lieutenant shrugged. 'How?'

'Order them.'

'Major-general, you have just given the order. They didn't obey.'

Sergeant Naso didn't wait to be addressed. He lifted his shoulders disdainfully and walked off after the men.

It was a frightful gesture. The lieutenant saw the sweat of shock and abasement form on the major-general's face. He should have pitied him: but he didn't. He holds our lives in his hands, he thought. He is not strong enough to hold them. He'd threatened to leave the Pirellis lying in a ditch. This was the moment to leave them. And he couldn't. He was too soft-hearted. He looked at him cruelly. This is no

Napoleon to lead the rabble from Moscow. He is just a passenger like the rest of us. He is nothing but a fat man in a uniform that didn't fit him before, and fits him even worse now.

'There will be courts-martial over this,' the major-general said in a lost, bitter voice. He wiped his face.

The lieutenant thought coldly: there will be no courts-martial. No rejected commander liked to display his shame. The men had disappeared down the road. The sergeant was turning the bend. He wondered how the situation would resolve itself.

Luigi's wife resolved it for them.

She uttered a screech like a choked owl. It staggered the lieutenant. 'Get up,' she cried. Her eye flickered like a lamp with a bad connection. She kicked her husband in the side. The lieutenant heard the thud. He thought she'd broken one of his ribs.

His eyes opened. He looked at her piteously. At least he was alive. His hands said: please. I am stricken.

'Animal,' she screamed. 'Get up. Do you hear?' She yanked him to his feet. He made with his hands: my legs are finished. She understood every word his fingers said. 'Walk.' She kicked him again. 'Or I will leave you to rot.' She hauled Sophia out of the ditch by the scruff of her neck. She slapped each side of her face.

'Mama.'

'Move. Both of you. Fall again and I will trample over you. I swear it.'

They began to walk. She stood glaring at them. Her dreadful eye batted madly. The lieutenant watched her with begrudging admiration. She is more of a man than our major-general. They all followed the distant figure of Sergeant Naso.

The major-general tried to speed up. He wanted to get back to the head of the column. It was his natural place.

But his feet were pulped islands of pain. He fell back. The lieutenant didn't wait for him.

The sun blazed. The boots went: crunch, crunch, crunch. The dust rose. Lips caked. The men trudged like zombies.

And then – at about three in the afternoon – the moment of the meeting came. The detachment and Caesar's cage were travelling along almost parallel roads. They joined. Caesar heard the lagging thud of boots and looked round. The men had issued on to the highway and were straggling fifty paces behind the cage.

He stared. This isn't much of an army, he thought. Big Julius would throw up. He saw Sergeant Naso a little way back. Then the lieutenant and the Pirellis. They looked ill. And finally, a long way back, the major-general. He was limping arduously. What a funny place for a commander to lead his army, Caesar thought.

XIII

SERGEANT NASO quickened his steps to catch up. He hissed under his breath. It was like walking on nails. 'Boy,' he called out. 'Wait a minute.' Caesar looked round calmly. He nodded. And went stalking on. The sergeant passed the two nuns. They were indescribably ragged and befouled. What, in heaven's name, had happened to them? He bowed gravely. They bowed back. He passed Maria. Her pale face gave him a pang. She was as grimy as the nuns. He winked at her. She smiled wanly and went trudging on. The sergeant caught up with Caesar and reached out to grab his shoulder. He opened his mouth to say . . .

'Well, I see you're still with us.' Caesar grinned slyly. He'd said it first.

The sergeant was put out for a moment. Then he grinned, too. Instead of grabbing Caesar's shoulder he rumpled his hair.

'That's right. We're still with you,' he said. He hobbled. 'What's your hurry? You're not catching any train.'

'We can't stop to talk.'

'Listen, boy . . .'

'Don't call me boy,' Caesar said. 'I am a man.'

He was even fouler than the others. His bare knees showed through his pants. The sergeant looked at the sharp undaunted face and chuckled. 'All right, then. Man. Listen, man,' he asked. 'What happened to your mules?'

Caesar shrugged. 'Dinner,' he said.

The sergeant was startled. 'You ate them?'

'I donated them to the starving poor,' Caesar said.

The sergeant could guess how they were donated. Forcibly. He wondered how Caesar had managed to keep the donkeys. This boy – sorry, man – could talk the Pope out of his tiara. He kept a straight face.

He noticed that one of the cages was missing. The donkeys tugged staunchly. He could hear their proud, straining breath. He gave them a butcher's look, thinking: I wonder how they would cook? 'I don't see your chimpanzees, either.'

'I gave them their freedom. They earned it,' Caesar said.

'That's a pity. I could have eaten them.'

Caesar's eyes glinted angrily. Sergeant Naso chuckled again: but this time to himself. Who'd have thought it? The boy actually has a sentimental streak.

'You've had a bad time, have you?'

'Nobody's grumbling,' Caesar said.

'I'm a soldier. You expect soldiers to grumble.'

'It shouldn't stop you marching like one,' Caesar said. And he turned to stare scornfully at the disorganized sprawl of the men.

It annoyed the sergeant. He stared round, too. They *were* rather a rabble. 'Straighten up ranks. Form double column,' he barked. He didn't see them take any notice. He might as well have given the order in Swahili. He stared irritably at Caesar and said, 'You don't look in such good shape yourself.'

'We're on our way. We carry two important passengers. I'm going to deliver them where I said I would. And nobody is going to stop me,' Caesar said.

'Big mouth,' the sergeant said.

'Big heart,' Sister Ursula flashed at him. 'Big spirit. You have no right to speak to him like that.'

The sergeant was astonished by her reaction. He rubbed his face.

'He's done wonders for us,' Maria said to him severely.

'We wouldn't be here without him. You should be ashamed of yourself.'

The sergeant was getting it from all sides. He wished he'd kept his mouth shut.

Even Mother Beatrice had to get her word in. 'You should be careful,' she said stiffly. 'He is young. He has done great things. I have high hopes of him.'

It was a little qualified, of course. She wasn't prepared to be too gushing. But it was a surprising admission from her. Even Caesar was surprised. He felt quite warm. I didn't think they appreciated me, he thought.

'All right, all right,' the sergeant said. He held up his hands. He was defeated. He dropped back and rejoined the men.

It mustn't go to his head, Mother Beatrice thought, watching Caesar. He needs humility. There is so much work to be done on him.

Maria thought calmly: I will marry him when I grow up.

He will turn out to be a blessing, Sister Ursula thought.

Caesar dragged to a stop. 'Rest,' he said to Castor. Pollux automatically rested, too. The cage clattered to a halt at the side of the road. Caesar was surprised to see the wavering sprawl of the men stop, too, as if they'd accepted the order unthinkingly. They dropped into the ditch. The major-general caught up. He was in great pain. He was angry. He was about to say, 'Who ordered you to . . . ?' but he was afraid of a public rebuff. He put a good face on it and sat tiredly in the ditch.

Caesar went round to see if God was all right. He was. The young face glinted. His mother seemed rested. 'Did you hear all that?' Caesar said to God. 'They want to make me meek. You know what they say. The meek inherit the earth. I don't think they do. I think the strong inherit the earth.' As he was speaking his fingers were stroking the marble under the straw.

He thought – somehow – God disagreed with him strenuously. He couldn't tell how. It was rather strange. Not a plaster muscle moved in the child's face.

'A man's strength is his belief in himself,' Caesar said. 'Can I help it if I feel it bursting inside me? What am I supposed to do? Choke it down? I am what I am. I believe in me.'

It was probably imagination. There was a kind of electric tension in the air. He seemed to hear an odd echo: believe also in charity, it said. Do not be too great in your own eyes. Make others great. Be their servants. And fulfil yourself.

That isn't fulfilling yourself, Caesar thought. It's just being nothing.

It is everything, the echo said. Or seemed to say. His ears rang. He felt that the virgin's eyes were curiously fixed on him. Be every man's brother, they said. Let them share your strength.

It was all rather terribly negative. Caesar watched Major-General Brazzolo removing his boots. Who wants to be that fat man's brother? He sat staring with horror at his swollen feet. That's silly, Caesar thought. You'll never get them on again.

He smelled the two nuns before he even turned. He wished they'd get out of the habit of eavesdropping.

'What did God say to you?' Sister Ursula asked softly.

'I don't get a word out of him.'

'He has just put it in your heart. Listen to it. Go over and talk to our friend.' She was watching the major-general with pity. He was trying to puncture his blisters.

'You can't talk to him. He just fights,' Caesar said.

'And you don't?'

'Self-defence.'

'Self-conceit.' Sister Ursula chuckled. 'He is in distress. Show him kindness,' she said.

'What for?'

'Didn't God tell you?'

'Not in so many words.'

'I will tell you his words. Love them that despite you.'

'He said that?'

'In exactly those words.'

Caesar stared hard at the major-general. He wasn't having much success with his blisters. 'He despites me all the time.'

'And you him. Now stop it. Once and for all. Go over. Offer to be his friend.'

'He'd hit me.'

'Turn the other cheek.'

'He'd just hit that, too. It'd be mad.'

'Try. For the sake of God. It could be yet another miracle.'

Caesar looked at Mother Beatrice. She hadn't said a word. But her face worked. She was in the grip of a very strong emotion. 'Go over to him,' she said in a dry voice. 'Give him your hand.'

Caesar felt – thought he felt – Big Julius jerk ominously in his fingers. He let him roll under the straw. 'All right. I don't think it'll work.' He grinned. 'You know what'll happen? I'll just get two cheeks slapped.'

He walked across to the major-general. He was still poking at his blisters. He stared at Caesar's feet. His eyes rose slowly. They met Caesar's. There was a dragging silence that was as bitter as a blow. Look, he's despiting me already, Caesar thought. Let's try to love him. How fat and unwholesome he is.

'That's very bad,' he said politely. He stared at Major-General Brazzolo's feet. They were appalling. He had never seen such swollen toes.

The major-general said nothing.

'You shouldn't have taken your boots off,' Caesar said. 'You won't get them on again.'

The major-general's eyes said bitterly: and that makes you happy?

I don't see why I should weep, Caesar thought. 'Let me help you,' he said. He went to the cage and dragged a blanket off the top. He tore it into strips with his knife. He came back and said kindly, 'You've a long way to go. This'll make you comfortable.' He crouched. The major-general watched him strangely as he began to bind the strips about his toes.

'Why are you doing that?'

'They must hurt.'

It wasn't the answer the major-general had expected. 'Listen,' Caesar said frankly. He went on binding the feet. He padded them so that each looked like an inflated canoe. It put the next thought into his mind. 'We're all in the same boat. We have to give each other a lift on the way. You'd do as much for me.' He didn't believe it for an instant.

He finished and stood up. The sun caught his bleached hair. He was dirty, but unbowed. The major-general stared into the calm grey eyes. He felt again that begrudging sense of loss: I should have had a son like that.

The feeling was so intense that it almost brought tears to his eyes.

'Let bygones be bygones,' Caesar said.

The major-general sighed. He tried his feet. They were more comfortable. He didn't think they'd last out the journey. But it showed kindness. Maybe I have been too hard on him, he thought.

'Is that better?' Caesar asked.

'Yes. Better.'

'Good. Not to worry. We'll come through.'

'I am sure of it.'

'It's just an experience. After all, we don't have earthquakes every day.'

'We have all been unlucky,' the major-general said.

Caesar patted his stomach. 'It's just being hungry that's bad.' He looked at the major-general's belly, thinking: I wish I had his reserve of fat.

'Boy,' the major-general said. He was quite moved. 'If I have seemed a little harsh . . .'

'Make nothing of it. I forgive you,' Caesar said.

The major-general felt his skin prickle. He forgives *me*?

'Love them that despite you.' Caesar looked round at the two nuns. They were watching him intensely. He hoped they were pleased.

The major-general had great difficulty with his throat. 'Did they tell you to say that?'

He's getting angry again, Caesar thought. What an inflammable man he is. He wondered how soon he'd have to turn the other cheek.

'We're in this together,' he said. 'Let's stay together and I'll get you to Rome.'

The voice seemed to come to the major-general from a long way off. *He* will get *me* to Rome? He thought he would burst a vein. 'We are going to Naples,' he said.

Caesar shrugged. 'You'll do better to follow me to Rome.'

He felt tranquilly that he'd done his duty. He held out his hand.

The major-general resisted the temptation to hit it. He said tremulously, 'Go away.'

'I'm sorry.'

'Go away from me. Before we are both sorry.'

'Did I say something wrong?'

'You have said nothing right from the moment I met you,' the major-general said.

I tried, Caesar thought. He studied the hurt, contorted face. What can you do with a man like that? He went back to the two nuns and said, 'Well, you saw with your own eyes. It didn't work.'

156

Sister Ursula's chest creaked with sorrow. 'You are sure you said nothing to provoke him?'

He searched his memory. 'Not that I can remember.'

Mother Beatrice's mouth tightened. She watched him narrowly. She seemed less convinced.

'Persevere,' Sister Ursula begged Caesar.

He sighed. They were good – but misguided – people. They were wasting his time.

'Return him affection for anger,' Sister Ursula cried. 'And thereby heap coals of fire on his head.'

She saw from the boy's face that he didn't know what 'heaping coals' meant. It was hard to explain. She had to go back to the original: Proverbs 25. 'If thine enemy be hungry,' she quoted, 'give him bread to eat. And if he be thirsty, give him water to drink. For thou shalt heap coals of fire upon his head.'

'Who said that?'

'Solomon.'

'I've heard of him. He was the wise one.' Caesar recollected that he'd had a great many wives. With some inkling of future sexuality he mused: perhaps that was also wise.

As he rested at the roadside he gave the 'heaping coals' homily a lot of thought. It intrigued him. Major-General Brazzolo had taken off his cap to fan his inflamed face. Caesar glanced at his scalp, thinking: it might be pleasant to heap a few hot embers on it. It wasn't quite the spirit of Proverbs 25. He stiffened. He'd been so absorbed that he hadn't seen a peculiarly dramatic situation developing. The men had been coming forward – individually at first, then in emotional groups – to kneel behind the cage. They crouched there, strung down the road, as more and more of them gathered, staring at the virgin, praying silently. The more volatile Sicilians touched her cloak with their handkerchiefs and pressed them to their lips. Caesar stared at them with astonishment. Then with irritation. It was he who had dragged the cage half-way across the mountains. He was getting to be a little possessive about God.

He heard Mother Beatrice catch her breath with pity. But her mouth had a curious twist. Caesar thought grimly: she knows that God is going to have to deliver. Which means that *I* am going to have to deliver.

Sergeant Naso came forward reluctantly to kneel with the others. Caesar shook his head. He'd always thought the sergeant a highly practical man. In fact, the sergeant was thinking: what harm can it do? It's just a kind of insurance. Not that it can do much good. Only food and strong legs can save us.

Major-General Brazzolo sat, nursing his feet. He wanted to pray, too. But he was an officer of field rank. He couldn't mingle his prayers too familiarly with those of enlisted men.

Caesar got up. He muttered to Sister Ursula, 'We're wasting time. We have to get on.'

'Presently.' Her eyes glittered with tears. 'They are praying for help.'

'Let them pray on their own time.' He almost added: and to their own God.

He thought: he doesn't want your tears. Can't you see how young he is? He needs a little help himself. She made him feel impatient. He walked away from her. Everything falls on me, he thought.

He scrambled up the bank. The valley stretched before him: ravaged as far as the eye could see.

It was as if a monstrous child had dragged its finger-nails across it. Nature had never been kind to the lower Abruzzi. It was all flint and scrub: even the sparse grass had a yellow dehydrated look. Now it was all bulged with glistening limestone, shoved up from below as if the devil had stretched in his sleep. The downrush of stone had ripped channels through the forest. The ancient drover tracks, the *tratturi*, that wound down from the hills, were obliterated like a brown web. Caesar wrinkled his nose. Heaven had no need to be so cruel; this is persecution, he thought. The scarred earth baked in the pitiless sun. Nothing moved. Nothing but . . . and Caesar suddenly narrowed his eyes.

He climbed a tree to see better. They were only specks in the sky. But he watched them for a long time. He wondered what interested the buzzards.

He wasn't going to tear the men away from their act of worship for half an hour. He shinned down the tree and unhitched the donkeys. He said casually to Sister Ursula, 'I'm just going for a little ride. I'd like to look around.'

He didn't say anything to Mother Beatrice. He'd somehow lost communication with her.

'You will not stray far, my son?'

'Not too far.'

'We cannot afford to lose you.'

He didn't think they could, either. Mother Beatrice would call it arrogant. Well, it's just too bad: ask God why he didn't make me a meek man.

He made the rope into a bridle round Castor's neck. He climbed on his back. He felt as mobile as a *caballero*. He said, 'Hup,' and trotted down the hill. He looked round. Pollux was following magnetically. 'One of you is enough,' he said irritably. 'I don't need an escort.' Pollux gazed at him reproachfully. It was like trying to divide Siamese twins. Caesar grinned. He thought he knew what they meant when they said: stupid as a donkey. 'All right,' he said. 'If you have to. But stay close. Don't waste my time.'

He steered for the specks in the sky. They wheeled, then descended like midges. He could guess why. He lost them when he entered the forest. It was a maelstrom of crunched branches. He pointed himself like a bird-dog. He followed his nose. The earthquake had tossed up cedars that had been seedlings when Big Julius conquered Gaul. Caesar suddenly felt the loss of the marble head. He was a good companion to have along. The donkeys mewed like nervous kittens. They hated the sighing breath of the haunted, chewed-up trees.

Caesar thought: it *is* a bit witch-like. And he was losing his way. He turned two points off the compass in his brain and came out of the devil's kitchen of the forest into the blaze of the sun. The flints, spewed up like a badly digested meal, turned the donkey's hooves. Pollux suddenly reared. There was a dead bird. Caesar wondered if it had died of shock: and why none of the little predators of the forest had eaten it. They had probably all fled. He would have eaten it himself if the flies hadn't been so busy at it.

He saw the buzzards again, nearer, and pushed on. He could hear their throaty racket. The donkeys seemed to drag. He saw Pollux's eyes roll. He caught it, too. It was the sickly smell of putrefaction. The village appeared out of the hollow. The stench nearly threw him back. He thought every buzzard in central Italy was there. They rose in a mad clamorous flutter as he rode through.

Caesar thought: one has to be hard. This is death, and death is part of life. He tied his handkerchief over his nose. He felt Castor jerk between his knees. The village had died days back, and nature's scavengers had been busy cleaning up. There was a dead child in a ditch. It hadn't walked there. The rats had channelled redly into the flesh. The buzzards had dragged and gnawed and fed; they weren't very tidy, and Caesar averted his head. The church – there was always a church – was rubble. Everything was rubble. And· everything was dead. Then a dog barked hollowly: something lived.

And then Caesar heard a familiar sound: the bleat of a goat. And he knew that something else lived. It came from a hillside farm. The farm itself had been folded into the earth. But a goat lived on somewhere. Caesar jerked Castor round and followed the sound. He found the goat perched on the cracked roof of a barn. It watched him defiantly like a cock on a dung-hill. It was a very old goat, but edible. It had a beard.

Caesar thought coolly: I should respect age. But I am going to eat you. And then he heard the grunt of pigs and saw three of them, fat and ponderous, in the mud. I have found a gold-mine, he thought.

He dismounted. The goat continued to watch him. It had suspicions. They hardened as it saw Caesar untie the rope. He made a noose. He said to the goat, 'Do not let us waste time. You might as well come down.' It was as high as it could go. He swarmed up over the cracked timbers of the barn. It backed away. He didn't need the noose. It leapt with a wild bleat. He leapt too. He caught its hind leg in motion and hung on. The thing scuffled and kicked. It had surprising strength for a very old beast. He roped its legs and it lay watching him balefully. He thought: you should have come down. It would have saved me dragging you.

He got it down. He tied it over Castor's back. It was as scrawny as Methuselah in his later years. 'Be quiet,' he said to it coldly. It wouldn't cook very well.

Now the pigs. His belly swelled at their succulence. They were sleepy. 'Get up,' he said. 'You are going to walk a long way.' He picked up a timber and smacked their hams. They grunted. He drove them on. 'Come,' he said to Castor. It didn't care for the smell of the goat it carried. The pigs lurched ahead. Pollux nudged them on. They walked over the hill. They would have stopped to root on the way, but Caesar wanted to eat, too. And the timber went smack on their hams.

They skirted the forest. He came round in a wide circle. He was afraid that he'd lost the cage and the army detachment somewhere up that ridge. Then he saw a white cowl, high up, with Sister Ursula under it, and she was waving. He flurried the pigs on. They were only half-way up as the

161

men came down in a rush. They lifted the pigs. They couldn't wait for them to walk. Sergeant Naso said after a long while, 'Boy.' He seemed to run out of words. He gave a heartfelt sigh. He felt the goat. He would have eaten it if it had been six times as scrawny. He gripped Caesar's arm. 'Boy,' he said again. 'You are lucky.'

'It wasn't luck,' Caesar said sharply.

'No. It was something else.'

'So long as we understand.'

'You have good eyes. And a smart head. You have a keen appreciation of unusual situations. You are quick to seize upon opportunity. In other words, you have a general's head on a recruit's young shoulders.' Sergeant Naso chuckled. 'Is that enough?'

'That's enough,' Caesar said.

'Good.' The sergeant patted him. 'Now come and eat,' he said.

The fire hissed: the meat spat. Methuselah the goat was hide and bones and entrails over the cliff. Gobbets of him roasted on a spit. He defied his butchers even in death. He simply wouldn't cook down. But the pigs crackled and dripped. The men were too hungry to wait for the hams to brown; they tossed pieces of flesh into the air to cool and rammed them gaspingly in their mouths. Caesar's saliva ran. The odour was unbearable. He let out two notches in his belt in readiness. He was surprised how much he'd had to pull in. Then Sister Ursula came over with his portion.

He felt suddenly sick with hunger. He shivered: he fell on the meat with an animal-like greed.

She looked at him with pity. It would have startled him. Nobody needed pity less. She sat beside him. She sucked a ham-bone delicately. She wasn't very hungry. She was never very hungry.

'Good,' he said. His lips were greasy with fat.

'Very good, my son.'

'Eat as much as you can. It'll be bad tomorrow.'

'There will be more tomorrow. The Lord provides.'

I provide, Caesar thought. He wasn't going to start that argument all over again.

Her face was like creased grey satin in the glare of the sun. She is almost finished, he thought. This journey will kill her. Tomorrow – the day after, maybe – she will blow out like a candle.

She knew what he was thinking. She smiled faintly. She wasn't offended. When my time comes I shall be ready, she thought. I hope that he is ready for his blossoming young life.

And she watched him with pride. He is a volcano of a boy. He will do remarkable things. She wished she could live long enough to see them. She put down the ham-bone. Her fingers trembled. At least, I have had a share in him, she thought. I have helped to make him into a blessing. Heaven has been kind. I am succeeding with him. He is learning that the fear of the Lord is the beginning of wisdom.

The emotion almost choked her. 'My son,' she began . . .

'Hush.' He wasn't listening. He held up his hand.

'What is it?'

'Look.' He was watching the major-general. He sat apart from the men, staring with the bitterest intensity at his feet. Lieutenant Arnolfo had just gone across to him with his portion. Caesar wished he could hear. He couldn't. But the major-general's face spoke louder than words.

'Major-general,' the lieutenant said politely. 'I have saved the best part of the loin for you.'

The major-general glanced at it as if it were poison. 'No,' he said.

'It is good meat.' The lieutenant was bewildered.

'I expect you to refuse it.'

'I do not understand.'

163

'You should have more self-respect than to accept anything from that boy.'

'The men are starving.'

'Nobody will starve. Tell them that I forbid them to . . .' but the major-general looked at the men, feeding like animals about the fire, and his voice was lost in his throat. 'There is no more military discipline,' he said, and turned away.

The lieutenant stared at him with contempt. He put the meat on the ground by the major-general's feet and walked away.

'That Solomon was wise,' Caesar said.

'He was?' Sister Ursula heard him chuckle. It gave her a momentary doubt.

'Now I know what "heaping coals of fire" on the head means.' Caesar nodded at the major-general. 'Look at him. He is burning alive.'

'My son.' Sister Ursula's face twisted with alarm. 'It wasn't what Solomon meant.'

'What else could he mean?' Caesar remembered her quotation. '"If thine enemy be hungry, give him bread to eat." Well, I have just given him meat which is better than bread, and it is choking him like gall.'

Sister Ursula said to herself: be calm. He is young. Enlightenment cannot come all at once. It will take time.

'I will remember that for next time. It is a good way of paying an enemy off,' Caesar said.

Mother Beatrice was watching them. Sister Ursula suddenly felt the need of her comfort. She got up and went across.

The men grew drowsy. They had eaten until they were almost sick. The sun was beginning to dip below the hills. Caesar heard them yawn. He saw them stretch out. Twenty minutes, he thought. Just a little nap. He felt exhausted too. He gave one vast yawn and eased his bones on the hard . . .

. . . and suddenly woke. He stiffened. It was dusk. There

164

was a solitary star in the sky. It was noticeably cooler. Only the major-general was awake. He sat frustratedly kneading his swollen feet. Caesar got up with a jump. He shook Mother Beatrice and Sister Ursula. Sleep with the aged is as shallow as a dream: they woke instantly with grey faces. He kicked Maria lightly. She was curled up like a cocoon. She licked her lips and shivered and rose. He began to hitch up the donkeys quickly. The noise woke the men. They watched him silently. 'Move,' Caesar said crisply. 'Sleep in Rome. There is a long way to go.'

One by one they rose. Sergeant Naso thought irritably: who is giving whom orders? He looked at the major-general. He said nothing. He shrugged and got up, too.

Caesar flicked the donkeys and led off. The cage rattled. God and his mother were in transit again. The men formed up dream-like behind. Caesar heard the slur-slur-slur of their tired feet. He looked at Mother Beatrice. Her features were set. She was in great pain. But heaven was moving her legs. Sister Ursula hobbled staunchly. She is paper, Caesar thought. I had better keep an eye on her. The first puff of wind will blow her away.

Then he glanced back. The cage rolled and hammered. The men trudged in the rear. And far, far back the major-general sat. He didn't stir for a long time. Then slowly and arduously he got up. He followed.

Caesar wasn't beyond a little twinkle of triumph. I have taken his army away from him, he thought.

The moon was a cold ball of silver in the sky. They had been marching four hours. They had entered the dark weird forests of the lower Abruzzi. The tall stalky trees peered at them from the darkness. There was no sound but the rhythmic scrape of boots and the ungreased squeak of the cage. It was cooler to march in the dark; they were moving well, without grumble; we can keep this up until midnight,

Caesar thought. It cannot be long before we begin to smell hope and civilization. Owls hooted in the trees. It was very eerie. It was the time of ghosts. The men moved like ghosts, too.

Luigi Pirelli's wife was immediately behind Caesar. He looked round and met the twitching basilisk eye. He thought there was a glint of friendliness and approval in it. He could have been wrong. He wasn't afraid of evil eyes any more.

And then, for the last time in his life, he felt a tremor of the earth. He would remember it far into his manhood as the bitter after-taste of a cruel dream. It wasn't much of a tremor. It was as if the devil were having a little, perhaps not quite malicious, fun. The stones slithered. It was unnerving. Nothing is so frightful as the insecurity caused by the slipping of the solid earth on which people live. It didn't last long, either. There was a creaking of tumbling trees. The swishing and the tearing went on in the forest. Caesar sharpened his eyes.

He saw it coming as a dark bounding shape. It must have been the oldest and the most brittle tree in Christendom. It broke like brick before it was half-way down. It came rolling on. It stripped saplings and tore heather and ferns. Then it was here: one bound off. Caesar's throat thickened. He gave Mother Beatrice a shove with his shoulder and she fell with Sister Ursula out of the way. Maria had leapt aside like a goat. The donkeys squealed. The stump of the tree swept on them barrel-wise and the projecting thorn of a root whisked at the wheels of the cage and split them like twigs. The cage literally jarred on to the road and God and his mother shook for a moment. That was all. Just two broken wheels and the barrel of the tree was gone into the darkness like a wicked old gnome.

Caesar sighed. His hands were wet with sweat. It had all been so sudden: what time have I had to sweat? he thought. He stared through the bars of the cage at the virgin. She looked dolorous in the moon. The child gleamed sadly. Nobody was hurt. But there was no more transport and the forest was dark and ominous and the moon was still as ice.

The men stood drugged. They watched for a while. They were almost beyond shock. Then the head of the column stirred. Their tired legs seemed to move on their own. They went dragging on down the road, passing the virgin and the child, glancing at them guiltily, but not stopping. Sergeant Naso went by. He was half asleep. Then the major-general at the rear. He looked emptily at Caesar. There was no malice in him. Just tiredness. They were all shades, vanishing slowly down the road into the darkness, and in five minutes even the slur-slur of their feet was gone.

XIV

THIS will pay no rent, Caesar thought. He licked his lips. He glanced at God and said in his brain: this is some predicament. Don't you think? Why did you do it? He looked at Mother Beatrice and Sister Ursula. They were watching him. Why me? God is there. Look into the cage. Ask him. Caesar could hear Maria's shivering breath. She would cry soon. Women always cried. The two nuns, perhaps not being altogether women, didn't cry. But the donkeys moaned.

They were men-donkeys. Caesar patted them. Men shouldn't cry.

He examined the cage. It sat like a crate on the black, wind-swept road. The wheels were splintered spokes. An iron rim had rolled off for ever down the forested slope. Who is going to carry you, God? Your mother?

Would a small miracle be in order? Somebody has to get us to Rome.

'It's all right,' he said. He didn't think it was all right. But something reassuring had to be said. 'We've eaten well. At least we won't starve.' It still wouldn't get them to Rome.

'It's so dark,' Maria said.

'Till tomorrow. The sun always comes up.'

'And cold.'

'That's just fright.' It wasn't. It *was* cold. The wind had a bitter nip. 'Lie down in the cage. Wrap up in the straw.'

'God likes a little company, my child,' Sister Ursula said. For a moment Mother Beatrice's face darkened: it suggested sacrilege. Maria crept under the straw and squealed a little as she rolled over on the marble head. Caesar took it from her. This was precious. He'd had no Latin education: he didn't know what *alter ego* meant. He only knew that the marble head was his other self.

'What now?' he said to Mother Beatrice.

She put her hand through the bars to touch the virgin's cloak. 'She has brought us so far. Do you think she will abandon us now?'

'I was thinking more about abandoning her.'

'Never.'

'It's a thought, though . . .'

'Never. It is why we set out,' Sister Ursula said.

He saw the two nuns' faces close up. Old as they were, they could go like stone. They're not much help, are they? This is some predicament, he said to himself again.

He went to the brow of the road. He stared down into the pitch of the night. The wind frisked bitterly about his pants. He tightened another notch in his belt. He looked back. Castor was watching him. Pollux leaned flank-to-flank against him. Caesar had never heard of homosexual relationships. He simply thought: they love each other. And thinking this, a glow that might have been the milky way, but seemed a little pinker, caught his eye. It was far, far down in that well of blackness. The more he stared at it, trembling in the bite of the breeze, the more it thinned and faded into the starlit glimmer of the sky. It was probably imagination: but it seized like a burr on his mind.

He said to Mother Beatrice, 'If you can spare a minute.'

'I am doing nothing. Of course.'

'Look down there.'

'What should I see?'

'Look. Follow my finger. You tell me what you see.'

'Stars.'

'Left. Look. You are not watching. That big tree, there. Beyond the branches. A long way off. Well?'

'Lights?' Sister Ursula asked.

'I think so.'

He meant: I hope so. I don't know what we are going to do without hope.

He made a compass line down into the blackness. 'There is something down there,' he said. 'A village. Something. But that isn't the moon. It isn't the stars. I shall go and see.'

Mother Beatrice gasped, 'It is so far.'

'Not on a donkey.'

'How will you find your way back?'

God will radar me, he thought. It was a dry joke. He didn't think the nuns would appreciate it.

'Make a fire. Keep it alight. Don't fall asleep. It'll keep you warm.'

Sister Ursula said faintly, 'Would it not be better in the morning?'

'I shall be hungry in the morning.'

'Yes.' She sighed. Hunger didn't catch her like that. This was a very ravenous boy.

'And there'll be no shine down there to look for,' Caesar said.

'That, too, is a point.'

'Then that's all right,' Caesar said.

He dragged brushwood down from about the boles of the trees. He searched for the matches that he was careful to keep dry. He started the fire with a little straw. The thorns crackled. The sparks leapt to the sky. Sister Ursula sighed as they caught. She crept close. Maria crawled out of the cage and came over to warm herself, too.

Caesar stacked a store of brushwood for them. It wasn't in short supply. He gave Mother Beatrice the matches. Sister Ursula would lose them. 'Keep it going. And listen out for me. Don't go to sleep,' he said.

'My son.'

'Yes?'

He hoped she wasn't going to begin some tedious argument.

'If I have not expressed my high regard for you, permit me to do so now.'

He didn't know what to say to her. He stood in the road, brushing ferns off his pants. For the first time in his twelve years he was embarrassed.

'You minimize your own goodness,' Mother Beatrice said. 'I have watched you. I am a querulous old woman. So is this religious object at my side.' Sister Ursula, thus referred to, chuckled. 'But your tenacity, your courage, your unfailing high spirits, have been an inspiration.' He didn't know he had so many excellent qualities. He still said nothing, watching the nuns intently. 'It has been a privilege to know you,' Mother Beatrice said, and pressed him to her robe before he knew what she was at. She smelled musty. 'Now go with God.'

'I thought I was leaving him here.'

'He is with you for ever.'

I hope he will not always give me so much toil and trouble, Caesar thought.

He bridled Castor with the rope. It was no use trying to separate him from Pollux. Anyway, a spare mount might be useful when one tired. They were really quite small donkeys. He climbed on to Castor's back. He measured the direction of the pink shine in that windy distance. He fixed it in his brain. He had a moment's uneasiness. It *was* a long, long way. The night was deceptive. Look at the shine of the stars. And what a long, long way off they were.

But worry doesn't mend a hole in the pants. It was another saying he had, like: this doesn't pay the rent. He slapped Castor's flanks with his heels. They went trotting down the road. 'Remember,' he called back. 'The fire. I have to find you. Don't let it go out.' He saw Maria, small and getting smaller, the white cowls of the nuns, the flare of sparks, and then the night swallowed them.

The trees closed in like a tunnel. He'd read about Gehenna in the bible: it couldn't have been a blacker night than this.

The donkeys' hooves pattered like wood. Owls hooted. And somebody snored. It grabbed at Caesar's brain. He didn't believe the snore. He stopped. Castor panted. Caesar tweaked his ear and said, 'Quiet.' He heard it again: the throaty rumble. He saw the men lying like discarded baggage under the trees. They'd gone hardly any distance at all. They'd just dropped with exhaustion. He saw Sergeant Naso's stubbled face, turned up blindly. He snored worst of all.

He walked the donkeys on softly. Luigi Pirelli's wife watched him. Seemed to watch him: she slept like a log. The terrible eye just twitched on its own in her sleep. He came on Major-General Brazzolo, lying apart from his men. He preserved the distinction of rank even in sleep. His mouth was pursed pathetically like a rosebud. He isn't much, Caesar thought. I don't know why I was so angry with him. For the first time he felt sorry for him.

He crept across. He felt gently in his tunic pockets. He found the major-general's wallet with its identity card. It might be good to carry some kind of passport, Caesar thought. The photograph on it had been taken when the major-general was younger and happier. Caesar grinned and took his cap. It would keep his head warm. He put it on. It collapsed over his ears. There was a strap and he looped it under his neck. He left the men sleeping, the trees sonorous with the mass snoring, and he walked the donkeys on a short way and then climbed on Castor's back.

He checked the shimmer again. He was still sure that it wasn't the stars. The road wasn't his direction. It was time to descend. He nudged the two donkeys over to the verge. They recoiled. It was as black as a well. 'Go on,' Caesar said. 'It's all right, I tell you,' and they looked back at him, reassured, and risked their hooves on the unseen gorse.

It wasn't solid. They descended in a mewing rush like betrayed kittens, hooves shoved forward bird-wing fashion to check the fall: banging from trunk to trunk, scratched by springy twigs waiting for them like spiteful pranksters in the dark. Down into the morass of wet smelly leaves, down over earthquake-shifted saplings, and without knowing it they trod over the old bole that had smashed the wheels of the cage. It would have done them a little more harm if it could.

Then there was heather. And rabbit-holes. And rough, tough grass that wound about their hooves and tried to trip them up. And finally the jolting of buried cobbles. It was an old Roman causeway. Legions hadn't marched along it for two thousand years. Caesar lay on Castor's neck like an unseated jockey, hissing at the scratch of the thorns. He was almost flayed. His bundle banged like a piston-hammer on his spine. He'd brought Big Julius along instinctively. He thought: he's heavy, but friendly. Perhaps the great *imperator* had passed this way in ancient times.

The donkeys slid to a halt. They looked at him reproachfully. It had been a frightful experience. He didn't know if they'd quite trust him again. 'No bones broken,' he said briskly. Not much skin left, either. He rubbed his scratched face. 'Accidents happen.' Haste and over-confidence sometimes made them happen. He'd been a little bumptious. 'Well, move,' he said testily to Castor. 'Standing here like statues doesn't grow potatoes.' It was a variation on: this doesn't pay the rent.

He felt the donkey shiver between his knees. 'Get on with you,' he said, ramming in his heels, and Castor gave him a hurtful look. If he'd been able to speak like Balaam's ass he would have said: you are very harsh. Both donkeys

173

groped on. Testing a hoof at a time. They'd lost faith in him. This is going to take all night, Caesar thought.

He got down. 'Look,' he said, addressing Castor's muzzle. 'You're being a great nuisance. We don't have all day.' All night, rather. 'You have to help.'

Castor's eyes rolled piteously. 'I know,' they said. 'But you don't understand an animal's deficiencies. You're fearless. We're not.'

'You have to trust me.'

Pollux's eyes chimed in. 'We love you. But we are only dancing donkeys. We are not very brave.'

Caesar took hold of Castor's bridle. He could feel the old cobbles bulging beneath the spongy grass. The Romans built roads to go from place to place. This one led somewhere. He dragged at the rope, following the ancient way. Here and there the cobbles vanished and he had to poke on with his feet until he found the lost, cold stones again. They were greasy. The donkeys slithered behind.

Caesar thought irritably: they are making me mad. The rope cut into his shoulder. He talked to them steadily and venomously under his breath. It made no difference. They were very unhappy. They groped like blind old men.

He stared into the well of the night. He could still detect the pink shine: he would soon lose it. The night wouldn't last for ever. Low down in the east was a faint grey glow. It gave him a cold shock. He yanked hard at the rope.

'Bastards,' he said angrily to the donkeys. It was a reflection on their paternity. He'd suffered the same smirch himself. 'Move, will you?' They resisted. He dragged them on. He knew he'd done something wrong. He heard Castor's hooves grind for grip on the worn stones. There was no grip there. They fell together. The donkey rolled over him. He smelled the wet fearful flesh, felt the donkey's muzzle pant in his face, the hooves threshing wildly, and thought: oh, God: he has broken my bones.

174

Castor squirmed up. He stood trembling guiltily. Caesar turned over slowly. He didn't think he could get up. His hip was numb. He rose, stage by stage, first on one knee, propping himself on his arms. Then got erect. He hobbled. He tried a pace or two.

Castor followed. Caesar struck him cruelly across the muzzle. He had never heard a donkey weep. He heard it now. 'All right,' Caesar said. He knew he'd been unjust. 'Now we know who gives the orders. Do as you are told.'

Castor sighed. You are going to kill us, his eyes said.

'Get along with you.' Caesar climbed on to his back. He couldn't trust his hip. I hope I am not lame for life, he thought. 'Move.' Again with the vicious heels. The donkeys ploughed on resignedly. They didn't resist him any more. It was as if they had put their fate in his hands. The cobbles descended steeply. It must have been hard going for the Roman Legions. Caesar wondered where they led.

He felt a hard spatter. He looked up and saw ragged clouds scurrying across the stars. They blotted out the pink glimmer. He was lost. Sitting one-sidedly with the pain crawling up his hip. He needed another saying: it never rains but it pours.

He heard the sound of the torrent before he saw it. It rumbled like a goods-train in the valley. They came stumbling, sliding, down the slope to the bridge. He saw branches hiss by on the grey-flecked river, swollen by fat mountain streams. The bridge was as old as the cobbles. The water ripped at the buttresses. It had a tired slump that wasn't quite right. Caesar didn't know if the river had done it, or the earthquake. He got down. He walked a few steps across. It has lasted two thousand years: it will last out our time, he thought.

And he beckoned to Castor. 'One at a time,' he said. He saw the donkey's eyes flash. Its instincts were all on edge. 'Come.' He beckoned again. It was the last spark of rebellion.

Castor came delicately across. Caesar moved ahead; he thought he felt the greasy slip of old stones. It could have been the vibration of the river. All we ask is thirty seconds. You have lived so long: hold on a little longer, he thought.

He saw Pollux preparing to follow. It was unbearable for the donkeys to be apart. 'Wait,' he said sharply. 'Didn't you hear? One at a time.' And Pollux waited. They were two thirds of the way across.

He remembered the bouncy motion of the roundabout in the square of the village of Lorenzo of the Angels. It was a curious thought to have. It was a curious sensation he felt. A quiet, tired subsidence, then a lift from the racing water: then the sagging of the parapet, stones dropping from underneath him, and there was icy water up to his neck. He was clinging to a stump of a buttress. It was all that was left of the bridge.

He shouted. He saw Castor threshing in the water. The river swept the donkey away. 'No,' Caesar yelled. It was a terrible yell of protest. He got himself, pain and shivering skin, over to the bank and stood knee-deep, watching the donkey struggling, receding into the distance. There was a moon for an instant and he saw Castor for the last time. The head reared, then was lost.

Pollux bleated. Caesar thought, weeping, I will remember that sound to the day of my death. The donkey leapt in to follow its twin. It was better to be together, even in death. Caesar shook. 'No,' he was shouting over the roar of the river, beating at the water, but there was nobody to hear. He dragged himself out. Pollux went without a struggle, hastening after Castor.

Then the moon was gone. They were gone, too.

Caesar stood there, dripping, tears bursting from his eyes. All he could feel was a suffocating guilt. The bundle on his back was weighing him down. He flung the marble head with a cry of anguish after the donkeys. He didn't know why he did it: whether it was the rage of despair or a tragic gesture of betrayal. Now I have lost everything, my friends and Big Julius, he mourned.

He squelched up the bank. The rain couldn't make him wetter. He looked down once at the mad grey river, then shrugged. He took off the major-general's cap and water rushed out of it. He sighed. It couldn't make him laugh. He pushed on, up over the hill, in the drizzle, without direction. Presently the rain stopped out of pity. A cold, but compassionate, moon appeared.

He heard an airplane. He couldn't see it. Then another. The drone hung in the air. He thought they were landing somewhere. He followed the sound. He saw the amber lights of the approach-path of an airstrip. It was a makeshift affair. He came down to it, watching the flea-specks of more aircraft, and walked round the perimeter. The army had established a temporary post here. There wasn't even barbed wire. He came to a wooden hut. There were soldiers eating inside. The clatter of spoons almost made him retch. He pushed open the door. There was a warm, soupy smell. The men stared at him. He stared back.

He still wore the major-general's cap. A soldier said in a startled voice, 'Boy,' and Caesar motioned irritably: he was sick of being called boy. He looked at the food on the table. 'I want to see somebody important,' he said.

XV

THE duty-officer was a Captain Rienzi. He had just rolled
into his cot to snatch an hour's nap when they rang him
from the guard-room. He thought exasperatedly: they must
let me rest a little. They do not regard me as a human being.
He was red-eyed from lack of sleep. He had had a very bad
three days. And he sat staring at the wet and taciturn boy,
oozing gently on to the office floor, thinking: something
tells me that today is going to be even worse.

He was the squadron adjutant. He dealt with duty-
rosters and aircraft dispatch. The army, which loves paper,
had taught him to deal with it systematically. The emergency
had destroyed all system. It had swept him off his feet.

The command-post had been set up under a lieutenant-
colonel at an hour's notice to ferry supplies into the disaster
area: and fly refugees out. The evacuation of the province
was almost complete. Supplies were now beginning to rush
in. The whole world had been moved to sorrow for stricken
Italy. There was American corn and dried eggs and dehydrated milk, blankets and medicines from the British,
French doctors and technicians. The command-post was
suddenly multilingual. There were Jugoslavs and Russians.
And the post swarmed with twelve great Boeings, a fleet of
British Beverley transports, and three naval helicopters.
Captain Rienzi thought tiredly: what this place needs is
an organization unit of the United Nations. And all it has is
me.

He continued to stare heavily at the boy. He wondered
what was needed to deal with him.

178

He had dragged the warrant-officer out of bed. Let some-body else lose a little sleep, he thought. The warrant-officer came in with a plate of hot pasta for the boy. He said to him, 'Eat,' and Caesar shook his head impatiently and said, 'Hurry. You're wasting time.' He was frantic with anxiety. He couldn't understand why he should still be hungry. It was only a few hours since he'd eaten goat up on the wind-swept plateau with the men.

It was still very dark. Aircraft droned in the night. The captain couldn't keep his eyes open. When I retire I shall sleep for six solid months, he thought. He told the warrant-officer the boy's story.

And then he whispered, 'I think he is a liar. I do not believe a word of it.'

The warrant-officer was of the Sergeant Naso breed. But without the long nose: just hard-bitten. He was tempted to disbelieve the boy, too. He stared at the major-general's cap. He examined the identity card. It was very odd.

'He says they are all up there?'

'A whole technical unit. Under some Major-General Brazzolo. Have you ever heard of him?'

It was a large army. 'No,' the warrant-officer said.

'And God, too,' Captain Rienzi said. 'God and his mother. Everything is crazy. I can't make sense of the boy. He says we have to go up there and rescue God.'

The warrant-officer ran his eyes over Caesar. He looks as if he's been through a grinding mill. What a mess he is, he thought. He wondered how he'd come by the weal on his head. There was only one sodden sandal. The other had been left in the river.

'Boy. . .' he began.

And Caesar said, 'For the last time. Stop calling me boy. You're beginning to sound like Sergeant Naso.'

The captain saw the warrant-officer stiffen. 'You know him?'

179

'I served with him in Greece. Everybody knows Sergeant Naso.'

Captain Rienzi didn't know him. He wished it was morning. The sun made the maddest things look sane.

'Dry him off. Give him a blanket. I'll refer the matter to headquarters,' he said.

'Now?'

'What's the matter with you? Do you know what time it is? It's the middle of the night.'

'It's very bleak up in the hills.' The warrant-officer shrugged. 'They've come a long way. They must have suffered a lot. We don't want any of them to die.'

The captain wrinkled incredulously. 'You don't believe his story?'

'I don't know. Where did he get the identity card? And the major-general's cap?'

'Ask God. The one who has to be rescued. The one the boy says is up there. I'm very tired,' the captain said. He screwed his eyes. 'I've had no sleep since Monday. What do you want me to do?'

The warrant-officer didn't believe in giving officers orders. He rubbed his stubble. He took a risk.

'Wake the lieutenant-colonel.'

'He'll shoot me.'

'It's a military hazard. People join the army to get shot.'

'Not me.' The captain was a desk-officer. 'Adjutants stay out of the firing line.'

'You could be right in it,' the warrant-officer said. 'There's been an earthquake. Strange things have happened. If it turned out that . . .'

'All right. I'll wake him.' The captain called the guard-room to ring the lieutenant-colonel. He felt suddenly uneasy. He made the message urgent. 'And I'll tell him you suggested it,' he said.

They're not very efficient, Caesar thought scornfully.

They should be doing something. And all I can hear is talk, talk, talk. No wonder I was able to defeat a whole Italian army. They're not the same breed as Big Julius' men. But *I* am, he told himself fiercely: I'm straight out of his loins. He shivered. The damp was eating like acid into his bones. He pictured Maria and Mother Beatrice and Sister Ursula, cold and lost, in that forested wilderness. It filled him with despair. And God and his mother, too. I have a terrible responsibility there, he thought. His head drooped. The warrant-officer, watching him curiously, thought: the boy has a tired old man's face. Caesar mumbled to himself drowsily: I have to get back to them. I must find Castor and Pollux. His eyes suddenly gushed tears. He'd forgotten in his weariness that they were dead. I have lost the best of my friends. The dying spark of his brain remembered them all: Lucrezia, Numbers One and Two, and the brave dancing donkeys. The warrant-officer, still watching with pity, wondered why a boy who was half asleep should cry.

He threw a blanket over his shoulders. Caesar didn't feel it. He didn't even hear the lieutenant-colonel come in.

He was young for a lieutenant-colonel. He was a bomber pilot. He had the hard, rather theatrical virility of his kind. He sported an eccentric clipped beard. His eyes, which he was trying to unglue, were like glistening brown nuts. He was in a bad temper. He hadn't slept much since Monday, either. He came in, dragging on his pyjama top. The lower half of him was naked. He said with one vast yawn to Captain Rienzi, 'You'd better have an excuse ready. And it had better be good. If it isn't . . .' then his eyes rested on Caesar, oozing a pool on the office floor, and he said softly, 'How did that *ragazzo* (Neapolitan argot for urchin) get washed in here?'

Captain Rienzi flinched. The warrant-officer kept his mouth shut.

'Don't you read Standing Orders? This base is forbidden to civilians,' the lieutenant-colonel said. He continued to stare at Caesar, sleeping heavily. He didn't seem much of a civilian.

'Sir,' Captain Rienzi sighed. He was frightened of the lieutenant-colonel. Caesar slept on. He didn't hear him explain. The lieutenant-colonel listened absently, fingering the major-general's cap, tossing the identity card from hand to hand. I must have been crazy, the captain thought. I should have thrown the guttersnipe out . . . then he was astonished to see the lieutenant-colonel nod.

'I know him.'

'You do?'

'Fat Brazzolo. One of the back-room boys. A radar genius,' the lieutenant-colonel said.

The captain hoped the warrant-officer would go on keeping his mouth shut. 'I thought it best to wake you.'

'I'd have had your ——' (a coarse reference to the captain's testicular organs) 'if you hadn't,' the lieutenant-colonel said. He poked at the sleeping boy. He stank of mud. 'Which of you beat him up?'

The captain was shocked. 'He came in this condition.'

'How did he get here?'

'He crossed the river.'

'He must be out of his mind. It's running a torrent. He came by himself?'

'He had two donkeys. He says he lost them in the river.'

'They must have been crazy, too.' The lieutenant-colonel went to the window. He watched a Boeing growl in. He peered into the darkness. 'He says they're all stuck up on that ridge?'

'Higher than that. Far back in the hills.'

'You think he's a liar?'

The captain didn't know how to eat his words. 'Yes.'

'No,' the warrant-officer said.

'We'll soon find out,' the lieutenant-colonel said. He gave the boy a hard shake. 'Wake up.' Caesar opened his eyes very slowly. It was as if his consciousness had had to return from Mars. The lieutenant-colonel touched the weal on his head. 'How did you get that?'

'It's a long story.'

'I have no time for long stories,' the lieutenant-colonel said. 'Where do you come from?'

'The village of Lorenzo of the Angels.'

'I never heard of it.'

I probably never heard of you, either, Caesar thought. He wondered who the man was. He stared at his private parts. It was hard to identify somebody who was naked from the hips down. 'It's on the other side of the Abruzzi.'

The lieutenant-colonel seemed startled. 'That's a long way.'

'If you go on wasting time you'll make it seem longer,' Caesar said.

'What's your name?'

Caesar told him.

'Caesar what?'

'It isn't your business.'

'A *bastardo*?'

'Say that again,' Caesar said, rising tiredly, 'and you will lose some of your teeth.' The lieutenant-colonel chuckled and pushed him back. The boy subsided wetly into his seat.

'How many men are supposed to be stuck up there?' the lieutenant-colonel asked.

'Not supposed to be. They're there.'

'Answer the question.'

'Do you think I'm a liar?'

'Probably. How many men?'

Caesar recited the roll-call. One major-general. A Lieutenant Arnolfo. Sergeant Naso. So many enlisted men. So many refugees.

'Any dead?'

'Two I think. If you wait much longer there'll be more.'

It's all a little too pat. He's a little too bossy, too. I may have to slap his ears for him, the lieutenant-colonel thought. 'Describe the major-general.'

'Fat.' Caesar painted the picture. It was very descriptive. 'Hot-headed. Big with the mouth. Like the belly. I don't think much of him. It wasn't too hard to run rings round him.'

It annoyed the lieutenant-colonel. 'Listen, *vagabondo*.' A shade more insulting than *ragazzo*. 'Watch your tongue . . .'

'Who are you?'

'I am the commander of this post.'

'Then why don't you do something?' Caesar shivered with despair. Half the night will run away while they talk, talk, talk. 'Try to help a little.'

'Not so fast. We have to be sure that you are not . . .'

'They are lost up there. They are cold. They are frightened. Hurry,' Caesar said.

The lieutenant-colonel watched him grimly. He could still be a liar. But I can't afford to take a chance. 'All right,' he said reluctantly. 'We'll see about fetching the men down.'

'God and his mother first,' Caesar said.

The lieutenant-colonel thought irritably: don't let's have that nonsense again. He had heard all about them from the captain. He dismissed them with a wave. 'God's been taking care of himself since the beginning of eternity,' he said impatiently. 'He can take care of himself a little longer. The men first.'

'No. God first,' Caesar said stubbornly. 'Then the men.'

'Are you telling me what to do?'

'If I have to. I know where they are,' Caesar told him. 'You don't.'

The lieutenant-colonel bit his tongue. I may have to break, say, one of the small bones of his wrist, he thought. 'Boy. Don't make me . . .'

'You don't frighten me,' Caesar said.

The lieutenant-colonel gave him a hard stare. 'What does frighten you?'

'Abandoning God. Breaking my word to him and his mother. I promised I'd get them to Rome.'

The lieutenant-colonel scratched his hairy thighs. Nobody would believe this conversation, he thought. 'All right,' he agreed. 'God first. I hope for your sake he's there.' Because if he isn't it won't be one of the small bones of your wrist I'll break: it'll be your shins and your skull. It suddenly occurred to him. 'How are we supposed to find them in the dark?'

'I told Mother Beatrice to keep the fire burning.'

'You thought of everything.'

'Yes,' Caesar said calmly. 'Somebody had to. You talk rather a lot, don't you? Get your army together. We've a long way to march.'

'Nobody's going to march. This is the twentieth century.' The lieutenant-colonel grinned. 'We go by helicopter.' He found himself begrudgingly liking the boy and he twisted his hair. 'Spread your wings a little.'

Caesar's heart leapt. He had never flown. Yes, he thought, passionately: from now on I shall spread my wings. The lieutenant-colonel glanced down at his nudity. He thought cynically: I mustn't appear like this before God. 'Come,' he said, leading Caesar out. The warrant-officer watched them go with a chuckle. Captain Rienzi thought: it will probably all turn out to be part of a dream. I must get back to bed.

A chill wind swept across the airstrip when Caesar emerged with the lieutenant-colonel. The approach-lights glittered. A fat-bellied transport came out of the night with a swish and roar and trundled down the tarmac. A helicopter was warming up in a corner of the field. A corporal sat at the controls. The lieutenant-colonel motioned him into the back and took his seat. He beckoned Caesar to his side. Caesar squashed in. It was like being in a glass bowl. He felt the gritty flicker of the rotors. He didn't want to show his excitement. It was almost more than he could bear. The machine swung lightly. It simply heaved itself like a bug off the ground. Suddenly the roar was deafening; the blades banged over the boy's head; and, looking down, he saw the dark field recede. The approach-path glittered off into the emptiness of the night.

They shot up. A tree loomed by and seemed to be blasted by the wind. Then they were too high up to see the flutter of the leaves and the tablecloth of the silent world slid by.

Everything was very small. Caesar searched the earth greedily with his eyes. He looked at the lieutenant-colonel, sitting sternly and professionally at the controls. Then he glanced up through the transparent roof. They seemed to be much nearer the stars. The whole vault of heaven blazed with them. Caesar thought: it must be wonderful up there. If that is God's home I'm surprised he bothers to leave it to come down here.

'Watch the ridge,' the lieutenant-colonel said to him coldly. 'You're supposed to show me the way.'

'I am watching,' Caesar said.

They were over the river almost at once. Caesar thought wryly: and it took me so long to walk. It foamed like a greasy streamlet. It gave him a moment's anguish. Somewhere in it, swirling perhaps in some scummy creek, Castor and Pollux lay. It didn't look so frightening up here. He couldn't see the bridge. Then the river fled and the trees reeled beneath them like corn, and suddenly the ridge towered: Caesar distinguished the ragged crest and pointed. 'There.' He was sure he knew it. 'Somewhere there.' The lieutenant-colonel gave him a cool look. 'Somewhere' wasn't very accurate. He pulled back and the helicopter lifted like a stuttering rocket and they soared over the ridge.

Caesar's mouth dried. He searched the gullies, dark and

ominous in the slanting glare of the moon. He could see the red-and-saffron flash of the false dawn. He thought: it all looks different. I was sure I knew every landmark. I tramped a road here, I fell down those slopes with Castor and Pollux, and suddenly – just like the donkeys – they are gone. He didn't want the lieutenant-colonel to see his anxiety. The lieutenant-colonel sensed it. And he gave Caesar another belligerent look.

'Do you see any fires?'

'No.'

The lieutenant-colonel said grimly, 'Neither do I.'

They went, higher and higher, up the wall of the cliff. The stone seemed as foreign as the craters of the moon. Caesar saw the white winding thread of a road. He looked at the stars, fixing a direction, and said, 'We came this way. I am sure of it.'

I am not so sure, the lieutenant-colonel thought. I am not sure of you, either. You are a liar. You will pay for it.

'Lower,' Caesar said. 'Follow the road.'

'I am still looking for the fire.'

Caesar stabbed down with his finger. 'It should be there.'

'But it isn't,' the lieutenant-colonel said. And I am soon going to start breaking your bones.

The fire was there. It was a grey nest of chilling ashes. Mother Beatrice slept beside it. Maria lay in her arms. Sister Ursula snored throatily. In her dream she heard the buzzing of a bee in the cage of her skull. She said thickly, 'No, no,' waving it away. She was afraid of bee-stings. She muttered in her sleep, 'Don't come near . . .' and lashed out at it. It woke her. She shivered. She could still hear the bee. It clattered mechanically in the sky. It swept across the ridge, right over her head. She glared at it with consternation. She saw a dark shape with skimming blades pass for an instant under the moon. She thought confusedly: something is there. The din was terrible. It receded into the valley and

Sister Ursula looked at the fire and shook Mother Beatrice agitatedly and cried, 'It is out.'

Mother Beatrice peered at her from her stupor. She heard the helicopter retreating. She stared guiltily at the dead fire. She gave a cry.

She got up. She rummaged amongst the warm grey ashes. She blew on them. An ember glowed for an instant. She piled brushwood on it hastily, fanning it with her robe. She stared wildly and pitifully at the sky. Then over at the cage. 'Mother of God,' she pleaded. 'Forgive me. What have I done?' And she blew and blew. There was almost no heat left.

She could hear the helicopter coming round. She ran to the cage and snatched a handful of straw. Sister Ursula flurried behind her with more. They stuffed it under the brushwood, fanning it again. The noise in the sky mocked them. The machine swung almost immediately above them: it passed with a thunderous racket, so close that they could almost touch it, and the blast of the rotors flapped their headbands.

Caesar sharpened his eyes. How dark everything is, he thought. I do not understand it. It should be there. He said loudly, 'I could swear it. I know the shape of the ridge. Somewhere there,' he cried, stabbing again with his finger into the darkness. But there was nothing there.

'Do you know what I should do with you?' the lieutenant-colonel said.

'Toss me out.'

'Don't tempt me.'

'I am telling you the truth.'

'I think you are a mischief-maker. You will not sit on your lying bottom for a month.'

Mother Beatrice said to herself bitterly: it is too late. She wept. She didn't know when she'd last wept. She put her hands together, like a medieval effigy, in an attitude of prayer.

I have betrayed my trust. She looked at the chilled fire, hissing faintly, and muttered, 'God, if we deserve pity, show it to us now.'

Sister Ursula seemed to wake out of a thick dream. She gave a cry. She ran to her bundle. She suffered with arthritis. She kept a small bottle of liniment to ease the ache of the flesh. She remembered that it had alcohol in it. She fumbled with the cork, tearing her nails, and dashed the contents into the ashes. A red spark glittered. It flared as if she had tossed kerosene on it. The straw caught. There was a vast whoosh of flame: it singed Sister Ursula's face and she leapt back with a jubilant gasp. Mother Beatrice stared at her with admiration.

Caesar said, 'Look.' He pointed. He saw for a moment a pin-prick of flame. He eased with relief into his seat. He was wetter with sweat than he'd been when he left the river.

The corporal in the back said hastily, 'I saw it,' and the lieutenant-colonel hoisted the helicopter about and flickered back. He saw it, too. He said to Caesar, 'You are lucky.'

'I have friends in heaven.'

The lieutenant-colonel gave him an odd look. 'Remember me to them. I could do with a friend there, too.'

He was almost over the fire. He could see the nuns waving in the red glare. There was a small girl dancing. He nudged the blatting helicopter away from the flames and touched down by them like a feather.

He stood for a long time staring at the cage, deposited like a crate in the middle of the road. He thought: this has to be seen to be believed. I'm not sure I even believe it now. He looked at the mother of God. He looked at the child. They looked at him in the pale glimmer of the moon. He wasn't at all religious, but he crossed himself absently. He pushed at the statue. It was only plaster; not very heavy. 'We'll have them down in twenty minutes,' he said.

'Good.' Caesar nodded briskly. I want to see you do it, his tone said.

'Now where are the men?' the lieutenant-colonel asked.

'I'll show you later.'

'Far?'

'Not too far. God first. Remember your promise. Then I will take you to the men.'

The lieutenant-colonel repressed his annoyance. He got busy with the corporal. They heaved the statue out of the cage. Caesar helped. It seems a long time since they first started the journey in it, he thought. They trussed it to two beams broken from the cage. It was a naval helicopter with an attachment for lowering life-saving gear: they roped it to the statue. The corporal took the helicopter up very gently. The statue rose and swung majestically in the air. It radiated the light of the moon. Mother Beatrice caught her breath. This is what miracles look like, she thought.

Then the helicopter roared and turned down into the valley. God and his mother flashed for a moment, hung on nothingness, then went miraculously off into the dark.

The lieutenant-colonel began to lace up long boots. He was getting ready for a long march. He had a first-aid kit in a valise. It rattled with two bottles of brandy. Caesar watched him thoughtfully. 'Now,' the lieutenant-colonel said to him. 'Lead the way.'

'It won't be necessary,' Caesar said.

'Boy. If you try to . . .'

'They're coming,' Caesar said.

The lieutenant-colonel peered into the gloom. A straggle of dark shapes was approaching. They had heard the racket of the helicopter. They had been just round the bend of the road all the time. The lieutenant-colonel stared sharply at Caesar. He felt an overwhelming desire to smack his head. He went forward to meet the men.

The major-general led them, his baby-lips pursed, his

round face shining, hobbling on swollen feet still wrapped in the strips of Caesar's blanket. The lieutenant-colonel didn't know what to say. A century ago, in a similar wilderness, Stanley had discovered a famous survivor and hadn't known what to say. He'd said instinctively, 'Dr Livingstone, I presume?' and for no clear reason the remark had echoed round the world. The lieutenant-colonel used almost exactly the same words. He went forward, saluted, put out his hand, and said, 'Major-General Brazzolo, I presume?'

XVI

FOR twenty minutes the crowds had been pouring into the Church of Santa Maria della Grazie for the dedicatory Mass. It is reached by a wide monumental sweep of stairs. Great Pope Julius had built it. Had it built, rather – there is a legend, probably unfounded, that Michelangelo had sketched it for him, but got no further with it because nobody saw to it that he was paid. The pontiff sometimes forgot that artists eat too. The church rumbled with music. The clear sexless voices of the choir soared above it like the chirp of birds in a storm.

Caesar felt himself swept gently by the throng up the steps, and when he reached the top he slipped aside, a little impatiently, from the gaping doors and sat on the ledge of an eroded statue of the prophet Jonah. He said to him politely, 'You won't mind me sharing your seat,' and let the crowds mill by him while he stared across Rome.

His eyes drank it in. The morning haze lay over the city. It softened its face. The little touch of magic wouldn't last long; in about an hour the blinding heat would raise every smell, coarsen every cracked tile, make the Forum look like something left unfinished after a strike of Roman masons in 50 B.C. Caesar thought: I must fix this picture in my mind. I will probably never see it again quite like this.

The piazza was alive; it whirled like a great coloured circus wheel about its hub. There was a kind of *passion* of motor-scooters and baby Fiats. The noise was deafening. By midday it would be insupportable. Every licence plate from San Francisco to Milan could be seen down there. A covey of nuns slid by chastely: priests with tureen-hats gossiped by a fountain. Some sea-god gushed water like a vomiting beast. Market-stalls ran off the old alleys. In Savonarola's time Romans had bargained here. It was mostly Americans who bargained here now. A *carabinieri* leaned on a hot-dog stand, munching *pizza*. Like Caesar, he watched the scene with pleasure. It was a little like a Puccini operetta. He was, too. He wore a tricorn plumed hat, red-striped trousers and a uselessly beautiful sword.

With one wide sweep of his glance Caesar could see six barber-shops. An Italian's hair is as much his pride as his virility. The barber-shop is also a refuge from women.

I had to come a long way to see it, Caesar thought. This is just the start. Rome first: then the world.

He'd been two days in Rome. The army had flown them all in. The nuns and Maria, the major-general and his entire unit. Not to Naples. Rome was nearer. Caesar chuckled reminiscently. It had been his last – the very last – victory. It didn't seem to matter much now. The nuns had fixed him up in a monks' hostel. Caesar found the cells bleak and the sparse food unfilling. After that terrible journey he seemed to be endlessly hungry. The monks had offered him fresh clothes, but he'd already sewn up his shirt and patched his pants. He said to the friar, 'You're very kind. But taking charity's a bad habit,' and the friar looked at him with shock. Dispensing charity was the business of his Order. This cut at the very root of its existence.

'My son, a little humility . . .'

'Why should I be humble because somebody offers me his cast-offs? Humility's a bad habit, too,' Caesar said. 'I came in my own clothes and with your kind permission I'll leave in them.' It was high time for him to go. He was wasting good days.

He made up his bundle. He got rid of a few things. He

kept the fairground-keeper's knife. It would remind him of the merry-go-round. He didn't need anything else to remind him of the journey. And he leaned back against the stone robe of the prophet Jonah, who'd also had rather a terrible journey in the belly of a whale. The bundle lay at his feet while he waited for the church to fill up, staring dreamily across Rome.

And then a voice said, 'Boy,' and corrected itself with a chuckle, remembering Caesar's objection. It was Sergeant Naso. He changed it to, 'My friend'. He gripped Caesar's arm. 'I wondered what had happened to you.'

'I'm fine.'

'You look fatter. You've been eating well.'

Caesar hadn't been eating well. He'd just slept better.

'Well, you're on your way,' Sergeant Naso said.

'That's right.'

The sergeant looked at Caesar's bundle. He tried it. It was lighter without the marble head. 'What happened to Big Julius?'

He saw a line of pain appear between the boy's eyes. 'I lost him in the river.'

'Better. Live your own life. Stand on your own feet, not on somebody else's. Listen, boy.' The sergeant couldn't get out of the habit. 'The army's a good career. Think about it. You might still wear Major-General Brazzolo's cap.' Caesar grinned. 'If you're ever in Naples look me up,' the sergeant said. He stared at Caesar. It was a little premature, of course. Say, in ten years. 'You'll find me in the Garibaldi barracks. Maybe with a long white beard.'

Caesar couldn't think why he should ever go to Naples.

'Good luck to you,' Sergeant Naso said, and went on up into the church.

Then Lieutenant Arnolfo. He wore a new uniform. He looked thin. Caesar wondered how this sensitive man had come to be a soldier. 'Well,' the lieutenant said gravely.

He touched Caesar's arm. 'I asked at the hostel about you.'

'You did?'

'They said you were too independent.' The actual word the angry friar had used was obstructive.

'I just left,' Caesar said.

'We should be grateful to you.'

'What for?'

'We owe you a lot.'

'Nobody owes me anything.'

The lieutenant said to him reprovingly, 'You must learn to accept gratitude. People have the right to offer it.' He suddenly realized that there was a vast gap between them. He found himself envying the boy his unbridled passion for life. He will grow up into one of the world's doers. I am just a watcher, he thought. He felt at a loss for words. He touched Caesar's arm again and said, 'I wish you well,' and went after Sergeant Naso into the church.

The soldiers of the unit came up the steps, one by one. Some of them glanced at Caesar and nodded. Most of them averted their heads. They felt a little guilty about leaving God and his mother in the middle of the road. They would say a few responses at the Mass and hope that that would make up for it.

And then, when almost everybody was in the church, a familiar fat figure: it stopped by Caesar with a jerk. It would have gone on if Caesar hadn't looked up. He hardly recognized Major-General Brazzolo. His uniform was very spruce. The leather shone. He carried a lot of beautiful harness for a desk-officer. He wore his decorations for the service. Caesar wondered with an inner grin: which war did he win them in? He was astonished to find that he felt no enmity for the major-general at all. It was as if he'd had a quarrel with somebody who'd passed only momentarily through his life and he couldn't remember what it was about.

He said simply, 'I'm glad you came. I wanted to say good-bye to you.'

The major-general looked at him intently. He couldn't trust himself to say anything. For the third – and last – time his heart creaked in his chest. He thought: here is a father-less boy. And I have to have three daughters.

'It was really all very silly. I hope we can forget every-thing,' Caesar said.

'Very well. I am satisfied,' the major-general said.

'We were all in trouble.'

Except that you made most of my trouble for me, the major-general thought bitterly.

'Do you think we'll laugh about it some time?' Caesar asked.

I sometimes wonder if I will ever laugh again, the major-general thought. He stared at the boy's candid face. It had betrayed him so often. 'What are you going to do with yourself?' he asked.

'See everything. Go everywhere.'

'Everywhere is a big place.'

'Not big enough for me,' Caesar said.

The major-general felt a strange wish for reconciliation. He wanted to say something nice to the boy.

'Perhaps we shall bump into each other occasionally while you are here.'

Caesar doubted it. He happened to know that the major-general was staying at the Hotel Excelsior. But he wanted to say something nice to him, too.

'I hope so.'

'You must see Rome first,' the major-general said. He was thawing fast. 'The *Città Santa*. The Holy City. It is a must. People come from every corner of the earth to see it.' He waved his arms excitedly. 'The army has given me ten days' sick leave. I am going to see it myself.'

'I'm glad,' Caesar said, and he looked demurely down his

nose. 'I did you a good turn, didn't I?' Something prompted the wickedly innocent remark. 'You never did get to Naples, did you? It had to be Rome.'

And the major-general flushed. He'd been unforgivably insulted. It was all over. He turned on his heel and went hastily up the steps into the church. Caesar watched the plump swaying bottom and the flashing harness, thinking: some people are very touchy. He never saw Major-General Brazzolo again.

If he were not to miss the service it was time to go up himself. He entered the church. There was no question of finding a seat; they were standing in serried masses all the way back from the nave. The air was cloying. The aromatic tang of incense stung his nostrils. He was suddenly uneasy; the smell brought back a memory of the church in Lorenzo of the Angels and the priest who was so quick with the clip about the ear. He felt lost at the back. He had to grin; he was, in a way, the *raison d'être* for this service. It was he who'd brought God home and he had to stand on his toes to see a thing. He squeezed in front. A plenipotentiary of the church in black tails gave him a glare. A Spanish bishop in purple jabbed his elbow at him. Then he burst through the standing mob, like tearing the rind of an orange, and he could see across the whole church.

The great dome was rich with pictures. They seemed more mythological than religious: there were flying angels and muscular saints gathered about a bearded personage like Jove. Everything was hot with the blaze of clusters of candles. The choir was brilliantly lit. There were a lot of nuns along the nave. He looked for Mother Beatrice and Sister Ursula. He couldn't see them.

His eyes swept the church. He couldn't see God and his mother, either. There were many plaster statues along the aisle. He suddenly found them: he'd been staring at them all the time. They were in a niche by the altar and he

197

could hardly recognize them. They'd crowned the mother. They'd given her a neon halo. It cheapened her. The child looked faintly cowed. Perhaps it was a trick of the light.

I don't think they're very happy here, Caesar thought. They weren't like that on the road. You remember the cage trundling and squeaking? The child glowing and the mother trembling encouragingly with love? I knew them better. I think I knew them best of all in those bad moments in the cave.

And he watched the priests re-dedicating the church to which they'd returned after five hundred years. He listened to the sonorous '*Domine, non sum dignus . . .*' and he thought: why do they have to talk to him so formally? I talked to God, man to man. Well, say: boy to boy. He sighed.

He felt out of place. It was suffocatingly close. The candles dripped wax. The Spanish bishop by him smelled like Luigi Pirelli and kept thrusting his elbow into his side. He shrugged sadly. I shouldn't have come. They've spoiled it for me, he thought.

Well, God, he said: this is where I leave you. I brought you a long way. We got to know each other well. I was fond of your mother. Perhaps she was a substitute for the one I never knew.

I don't know if you'll like it here. Imprisoned for ever in this austere place. It must be very lonely at night in the candlelight. It was better in the cage. Still, I did what I promised. I got you home. I hope you'll remember it sometime. I may have to come to you for a favour when I grow up.

And then the choir burst into the *Adeste Fidelis*. A boy sang a canticle and the buoyant silvery voice soared to the pictures on the dome. Suddenly Caesar saw God looking straight at him. The child's head was cocked: it was probably another trick of the light. The candles were causing all sorts of illusions. The mother, just for an instant, turned her eyes in his direction: they were so intent on him, so meaningful, that Caesar hung there irresolutely, squeezed between the plenipotentiary and the Spanish bishop, waiting for her to say something. Then a gust flickered the candles and the illusion was over.

Caesar turned to leave. He saw Mother Beatrice and Sister Ursula just at that moment. He didn't know why, in that great throng, they should suddenly see him. Mother Beatrice put her hand to her mouth with a spasm of recognition and beckoned to him as if to say: what is it? Why do you have to go?

The smell of the incense was fetching back in a bitter rush the cloying stench of the broken village of Lorenzo of the Angels, the memory of the priest with the hard hands, Luigi Pirelli with the talking fingers and the wife with the twitching eye; all the things he wanted to forget. Even the magistrate who'd been kind to him. For some strange reason he suddenly remembered the pale dead hand dangling out of the bed. He had to escape them. He went quickly out into the sunshine.

He knew that Mother Beatrice and Sister Ursula were moving after him. They caught up with him on the steps. Maria was with them. He'd never seen her so well-washed. She was hygienically unreal.

'Must you go?' Mother Beatrice seized his arm.

'This is just a waste of time.'

She gasped. 'Waste of *time*? You are in the presence of . . .'

'I know whose presence I'm in. I was in it all the way on the road. I had him to myself. It was very private.' He looked back at the church. 'Now they all want to share him. I don't like sharing things with people,' he said.

Mother Beatrice shivered. She'd lost him. It was going

to be lonely. Sister Ursula gave her arm a compassionate squeeze.

'Where are you going?'

'Down there.' He pointed across the piazza. 'I have to make my way in life.'

Maria said sternly, 'You're always in a hurry.'

'There's a lot to be done.'

'I don't know if I can trust you on your own. Do you want me to come with you?'

He looked at her cryptically. He travels fastest who travels alone. 'No,' he said.

'When will you be back? I'm going to marry you when I grow up.'

He doubted it. 'I've no time for marriage. A wife and children hold a man back.'

'Please yourself,' she said indifferently. She wanted to hear the music, anyway. She went back into the church.

'When shall we see you again?' Sister Ursula asked.

'Soon,' Caesar said.

Probably never. His life would be a lot of chapters. One had just ended. He was ready to turn the pages of the next.

'You know where to find us.'

'Yes.'

Mother Beatrice caught him to her. She still smelled musty: he supposed it was the quality of age. Then Sister Ursula. It embarrassed him. She smelled the same. He went down the steps. He heard Sister Ursula call after him, 'God go with you,' and he thought: why not? It helps to have friends in heaven. They watched him cross the piazza, dodging a motor-scooter. Saying something to the operatic *carabinieri* still munching *pizza* from the hot-dog stand. He circled the fountain with the sea-god that had been vomiting water for three hundred years. It wasn't hard to follow him. His was the only fair head in the crowd. He didn't turn. They'd half hoped he would wave.

He vanished amongst the market-stalls of one of the alleys.

Mother Beatrice's eyes grew bleak. Her heart was empty. Sister Ursula mumbled. They moved instinctively towards each other for comfort. And then they both went back into the church.